D1497933

MORE TALES
TO TREMBLE BY

More Tales To Tremble By

*A second collection of great stories
of haunting and suspense*

Edited by

Stephen P. Sutton

Illustrated by Gordon Laite

WHITMAN PUBLISHING DIVISION

WESTERN PUBLISHING COMPANY, INC., RACINE, WISCONSIN

ACKNOWLEDGMENTS

"The Red Lodge" by H. Russell Wakefield. From *They Return at Evening* by H. Russell Wakefield. Copyright 1928, D. Appleton and Company. Copyright renewed 1956, by H. Russell Wakefield. Reprinted by permission of Appleton-Century, affiliate of Meredith Press.

"Sredni Vashtar" by Saki. From *The Complete Short Stories of Saki* (H. H. Munro). All Rights Reserved. Reprinted by permission of The Viking Press, Inc., and The Bodley Head Ltd.

"Thurnley Abbey" by Perceval Landon. From *Raw Edges* by Perceval Landon. Reprinted by permission of William Heinemann Ltd.

"God Grante That She Lye Stille" by Cynthia Asquith. Copyright 1947, by Cynthia Asquith. By permission of Arkham House.

"The Voice in the Night" by William Hope Hodgson. Copyright 1914, by William Hope Hodgson. Copyright 1967, by August Derleth. By permission of Arkham House.

"The Extra Passenger" by August Derleth. Copyright 1946 by *Weird Tales*, 1953 by August Derleth. By permission of Arkham House.

"Casting the Runes" by M. R. James. From *The Collected Ghost Stories of M. R. James*. Reprinted by permission of Edward Arnold (Publishers) Ltd.

"The Book" by Margaret Irwin. Reprinted by permission of A. D. Peters & Co.

Library of Congress Catalog Card Number: 68-25322

CONTENTS

A Word to Midnight Readers

> Wizards know their times:
> Deep night, dark night, the silent of the night,
> The time of night when Troy was set on fire;
> The time when screech-owls cry and bandogs howl,
> And spirits walk and ghosts break up their graves.
>
> II HENRY VI, Act 1, sc. 4

Is THIS YOUR time of night? Are you most comfortable near midnight, when the shadows darken in the corners and the wind mutters through the eaves?

You are? Good! For this book is designed for lovers of "the very witching time of night."

You know, of course, that you may be facing considerable danger as you read the following pages. Edgar Allan Poe once said:

> Alas! the grim legion of sepulchral terrors cannot be regarded as altogether fanciful . . . they must sleep, or they will devour us; they must be suffered to slumber or we perish.

This might be putting it a little strongly, you say. After all, this is only a book, a collection of totally imaginary stories. But is it? We never really know where authors get the ideas for their ghost stories. Perhaps it *is* all imagination; on the other hand, maybe there is a basis in fact—perhaps even a personal experience—from which each story grew. If this is true, would it not be possible that in the retelling these "sepulchral terrors" might be called up from their grim vaults? And no matter how willing we are to face these horrors in our imagination, how ready are we to face them in reality?

Impossible? Consider this: Suppose an author (or an editor) with a certain knowledge and command of the supernatural, and a grim sense of humor, incorporated a special formula in his work—a formula that when studied, however unknowingly, at a certain time of night, under a certain conjunction of the stars, would cause the creature or thing in the story to rise before the reader.

Preposterous? Perhaps, but let us survey the creatures that could shortly appear before you.

First there is the creeping green thing in Wakefield's "The Red Lodge," who is in turn probably related to the dry, disinterred bones that rattle down the ancient halls of Landon's "Thurnley Abbey."

If the great god Sredni Vashtar appears before you, just hope that his passing is more pleasant than in Saki's story of the same title. And how would you feel with a lich sitting next to you? Even if you don't know what a lich is now, you would easily recognize one, as did the terrified hero of Derleth's "The Extra Passenger."

Do you like mushrooms on your steak or on your pizza? That will change after the fungoid creature in Hodgson's "A Voice in the Night" oozes onto your footstool.

"God Grante that She Lye Stille"—an interesting title for Cynthia Asquith's story, and even more interesting as the epitaph inscribed on Elspeth Clewer's moldering tombstone. Is this supplication for the comfort of the dead—or the living?

Approach M. R. James's story, "Casting the Runes," with special caution. The good Dr. James was a noted scholar of obscure ancient and medieval lore. He, perhaps more than any of the other authors in this book, would have had the necessary knowledge to play the little joke mentioned above. Wouldn't it be amusing to find that you have inadvertently cast the runes upon yourself—just as a strange shadow darkens your lamp?

Finally, and most ironically, Margaret Irwin's story, "The Book," deals with the possession of a man by a book—an evil, ancient, crumbling manuscript with a musty, tomblike smell. Our book has none of these qualities, of course—but still, we refuse to be responsible for anything that happens when you read *More Tales to Tremble By*.

Stephen P. Sutton

The Red Lodge

H. Russell Wakefield

I AM WRITING this from an imperative sense of duty, for I consider The Red Lodge is a foul deathtrap and utterly unfit to be a human habitation—it has its own proper denizens—and because I know its owner to be an unspeakable blackguard to allow it so to be used for his financial advantage. He knows the perils of the place perfectly well; I wrote him of our experiences, and he didn't even acknowledge the letter, and two days ago I saw the ghastly pesthouse advertised in *Country Life*. So anyone who rents The Red Lodge in the future will receive a copy of this document as well as some uncomfortable words from Sir William, and that scoundrel Wilkes can take what action he pleases.

I certainly didn't carry any prejudice against the place down to it with me: I had been too busy to look over it myself, but my wife reported extremely favorably—I take her word for most things—and I could tell by the photographs that it was a magnificent specimen of the medium-sized Queen Anne house, just the ideal thing for me. Mary said the garden was perfect, and there was the river for Tim

15

at the bottom of it. I had been longing for a holiday and was in the highest spirits as I traveled down. I was not in the highest spirits for long.

My first vague, faint uncertainty came to me so soon as I had crossed the threshold. I am a painter by profession and therefore sharply responsive to color tone. Well, it was a brilliantly fine day, and the hall of The Red Lodge was fully lighted, yet it seemed a shade off the key, as it were, as though I were regarding it through a pair of slightly darkened glasses. Only a painter would have noticed it, I fancy.

When Mary came out to greet me, she was not looking as well as I had hoped, or as well as a week in the country should have made her look.

"Everything all right?" I asked.

"Oh, yes," she replied, but I thought she found it difficult to say so, and then my eye detected a curious little spot of green on the maroon rug in front of the fireplace. I picked it up—it seemed like a patch of river slime.

"I suppose Tim brings those in," said Mary. "I've found several; of course, he swears he doesn't." And then for a moment we were silent, and a very unusual sense of constraint seemed to set a barrier between us. I went out into the garden to smoke a cigarette before lunch and sat myself down under a very fine mulberry tree.

I wondered if, after all, I had been wise to have left it all to Mary. There was nothing wrong with the house, of course, but I am a bit psychic, and I always know the mood or character of a house. One welcomes you with the tail-writhing enthusiasm of a really nice dog, makes you at home and at your ease at once. Others are sullen, watchful, hostile, with things to hide. They make you feel that you have obtruded yourself into some curious affairs which are none of your business. I had never encountered so hostile, aloof, and secretive a living place as The Red Lodge seemed when I first entered it. Well, it couldn't be helped, though it was disappointing; and there was Tim coming back from his walk, and the luncheon gong. My son seemed a little subdued and thoughtful, though he looked pretty well, and soon we were all chattering away with those quick changes of key which occur when the respective ages of the conversationalists are forty, thirty-three, and six and one-half, and after half a bottle of Meursault and a glass of port I began to think I had been a morbid ass. I was still so thinking when I began my holiday in the best possible way by going to sleep in an exquisitely comfortable chair under the mulberry tree. But I have slept better. I dozed off, but I had a silly impression of being watched, so that I kept waking up in case there might be someone with his eye on me. I was lying back and could just see a window on the second floor framed by a gap in the leaves, and on one occasion, when I woke rather sharply from one of these dozes, I thought I saw for a moment a face peering down at me, and this face seemed curiously flattened against the pane—just a carry-over from a dream, I concluded. However, I didn't feel like sleeping anymore and began to explore the garden. It was completely walled in, I found, except at the far end, where there was a door leading through to a path which, running parallel to the right-hand wall, led to the river a few yards away. I noticed on this door several of those patches of green slime for which Tim was supposedly responsible. It was a dark little corner cut off from the rest of the garden by two rowan trees, a cool, silent little place I thought it. And then it was time for Tim's cricket lesson, which was interrupted by the arrival of some infernal callers. But they were pleasant people, as a matter of fact, the local knuts, I gathered, who owned the Manor House—Sir William Prowse and his lady and his daughter. I went for a walk with him after tea.

"Who had this house before us?" I asked.

"People called Hawker," he replied. "That was two years ago."

"I wonder the owner doesn't live in it," I said. "It isn't an expensive place to keep up."

Sir William paused as if considering his reply.

"I think he dislikes being so near the river. I'm not sorry, for I detest the fellow. By the way, how long have you taken it for?"

"For three months," I replied. "Till the end of October."

"Well, if I can do anything for you I shall be delighted. If you are in any trouble, come straight to me." He slightly emphasized the last sentence.

I rather wondered what sort of trouble Sir William envisaged for me. Probably he shared the general opinion that artists were quite mad at times, and that when I had one of my lapses I should destroy the peace in some manner. However, I was duly grateful.

I was sorry to find Tim didn't seem to like the river; he appeared nervous of it, and I determined to help him to overcome this, for the fewer terrors one carries through life with one the better, and they can often be laid by delicate treatment in childhood. Curiously enough, the year before at Frinton he seemed to have no fear of the sea.

The rest of the day passed uneventfully—at least I think I can say so. After dinner I strolled down to the end of the garden, meaning to go through the door and have a look at the river. Just as I got my hand on the latch there came a very sharp, furtive whistle. I turned round quickly, but seeing no one, concluded it had come from someone in the lane outside. However, I didn't investigate further but went back to the house.

I woke up the next morning feeling a shade depressed. My dressing room smelled stale and bitter, and I flung its windows open. As I did so I felt my right foot slip on something. It was one of those small, slimy, green patches. Now, Tim would never come into my dressing room. An annoying little puzzle. How on earth had that patch . . . ? The question kept forcing its way into my mind as I dressed. How could a patch of green slime . . . ? How could a patch of green slime . . . ? Dropped from something? From what? I am very fond of my wife—she slaved for me when I was poor and always has kept me happy, comfortable, and faithful, and she gave me my small son Timothy. I must stand between her and patches of green slime! What in hell's name was I talking about? And it was a flamingly fine day. Yet all during breakfast my mind was trying to find some sufficient reason for these funny little patches of green slime, and not finding it.

After breakfast I told Tim I would take him out in a boat on the river.

"Must I, Daddy?" he asked, looking anxiously at me.

"No, of course not," I replied a trifle irritably, "but I believe you'll enjoy it."

"Should I be a funk if I didn't come?"

"No, Tim, but I think you should try it once, anyway."

"All right," he said.

He's a plucky little chap and did his very best to pretend to be enjoying himself, but I saw it was a failure from the start.

Perplexed and upset, I asked his nurse if she knew of any reason for this sudden fear of water.

"No, sir," she said. "The first day he ran down to the river just as he used to run down to the sea, but all of a sudden he started crying and ran back to the house. It seemed to me he'd seen something in the water which frightened him."

We spent the afternoon motoring round the neighborhood, and already I found a faint distaste at the idea of returning to the house, and again I had the impression that we were intruding, and that something had been going on during our absence which our return had interrupted.

Mary, pleading a headache, went to bed soon after dinner, and I went to the study to read.

As soon as I had shut the door I had again that very unpleasant sensation of being watched. It made the reading of Sidgwick's *The Use of Words in Reasoning*—an old favorite of mine, which requires concentration—a difficult business. Time after time I found myself peeping into dark corners and shifting my position. And there were little sharp sounds; just the oak paneling cracking, I supposed. After a time I became more absorbed in the book and less fidgety, and then I heard a very soft cough just behind me. I felt little icy rays pour down and through me, but I would *not* look around, and I *would* go on reading. I had just reached the following passage: "However many things may be said about Socrates or about any fact observed, there remains still more that might be said if the need arose; the need is the determining factor. Hence the distinction between complete and incomplete description, though perfectly sharp and clear in the abstract, can only have a meaning—can only be applied to actual cases—if it be taken as equivalent to *sufficient* description, the sufficiency being relative to some purpose. Evidently the description of Socrates as a man, scanty though it is, may be fully sufficient for the purpose of the modest inquiry whether he is *mortal* or not"—when my eye was caught by a green patch which suddenly appeared on the floor beside me, and then another and another, following a straight line toward the door. I picked up the nearest one, and it was a bit of soaking slime. I called on all my willpower, for I feared something worse to come, and it should *not* materialize—and then no more patches appeared. I got up and walked deliberately, slowly, to the door, turned on the light in the middle of the room, and then came back and turned out the reading lamp and went to my dressing room. I sat down and thought things over. There was something very wrong with this house. I had passed the stage of pretending otherwise, and my inclination was to take my family away from it the next day. But that meant sacrificing one hundred and sixty-eight pounds, and we had nowhere else to go. It was conceivable that these phenomena were perceptible only to me, being half a Highlander. I might be able to stick it out if I were careful and kept my tail up, for apparitions of this sort are partially subjective—one brings something of oneself to their materialization. That is a hard saying, but I believe it to be true. If Mary and Tim and the servants were immune it was up to me to face and fight this nastiness. As I undressed, I came to the decision that I would decide nothing then and there, and that I would see what happened. I made this decision against my better judgment, I think.

In bed I tried to thrust all this away from me by a conscious effort to "change the subject," as it were. The easiest subject for me to switch over to is the myriad-sided, useless, consistently abused business of creating things: stories out of pens and ink and

paper; representations of things and moods out of
paint, brushes, and canvas; and our own miseries,
perhaps, out of wine, women, and song. With a considerable effort, therefore, and with the edges of
my brain anxious to be busy with bits of green slime,
I recalled an article I had read that day on a glorious
word, *"Jugendbewegung,"* the "Youth Movement,"
that pregnant or merely wind-swollen Teutonism!
How ponderously it attempted to canonize with its
polysyllabic sonority that inverted Boy-Scoutishness
of the said youths and maidens. "One bad, mad deed
—sonnet—scribble of some kind—lousy daub—a day."
Bunk without spunk, sauce without force, futurism
without a past, merely a *transition* from one yelping
pose to another. And then I suddenly found myself at
the end of the garden, attempting desperately to hide
myself behind a rowan tree, while my eyes were held
relentlessly to face the door. And then it began slowly
to open, and something which was horridly unlike
anything I had seen before began passing through it,
and *I* knew It knew I was there, and then my head
seemed to burst and flamed asunder, splintered and
destroyed, and I awoke, trembling, to feel that something in the darkness was poised an inch or two above
me, and then drip, drip, drip, something began falling on my face. Mary was in the bed next to mine,
and I *would not* scream, but flung the clothes over
my head, my eyes streaming with the tears of terror.
And so I remained cowering till I heard the clock
strike five, and dawn, the ally I longed for, came,
and the birds began to sing, and then I slept.

I awoke a wreck, and after breakfast, feeling the need to be alone, I pretended I wanted to sketch and went out into the garden. Suddenly I recalled Sir William's remark about coming to see him if there was any trouble. Not much difficulty in guessing what he had meant. I'd go and see him about it at once. I wished I knew whether Mary was troubled, too. I hesitated to ask her, for if she were not, she was certain to become suspicious and uneasy if I questioned her. And then I discovered that while my brain had been busy with its thoughts my hand had also not been idle, but had been occupied in drawing a very singular design on the sketching block. I watched it as it went automatically on. Was it a design or a figure of some sort? When had I seen something like it before? My God, in my dream last night! I tore it to pieces and got up in agitation and made my way to the Manor House along a path through tall, bowing, stippled grasses hissing lightly in the breeze. My inclination was to run to the station and take the next train to anywhere; pure undiluted panic—an insufficiently analyzed word—that which causes men to trample on women and children when Death is making his choice. Of course, I had Mary and Tim and the servants to keep me from it, but supposing they had no claim on me, should I desert them? No, I should not. Why? Such things aren't done by respectable inhabitants of Great Britain—a people despised and respected by all other tribes. Despised as Philistines, but it took the jawbone of an ass to subdue that hardy race! Respected for what?

Birkenhead stuff. No, not the noble lord, for there
were no glittering prizes for those who went down
to the bottom of the sea in ships. My mind deliberately restricting itself to such highly debatable jingoism,
I reached the Manor House, to be told that Sir
William was up in London for the day but would
return that evening. Would he ring me up on his
return? "Yes, sir." And then, with lagging steps, back
to The Red Lodge.

I took Mary for a drive in the car after lunch.
Anything to get out of the beastly place. Tim didn't
come, as he preferred to play in the garden. In the
light of what happened, I suppose I shall be criticized
for leaving him alone with a nurse, but at that time
I held the theory that these appearances were in no
way malignant, and that it was more than possible
that even if Tim did see anything he wouldn't be
frightened, not realizing it was out of the ordinary in
any way. After all, nothing that I had seen or heard,
at any rate during the daytime, would strike him as
unusual.

Mary was very silent, and I was beginning to feel
sure, from a certain depression and oppression in her
manner and appearance, that my trouble was hers.
It was on the tip of my tongue to say something, but
I resolved to wait until I had heard what Sir William
had to say. It was a dark, somber, and brooding afternoon, and my spirits fell as we turned for home.
What a home!

We got back at six, and I had just stopped the
engine and helped Mary out when I heard a scream

from the garden. I rushed round to see Tim, his hands to his eyes, staggering across the lawn, the nurse running behind him. And then he screamed again and fell. I carried him into the house and laid him down on a sofa in the drawing room, and Mary went to him. I took the nurse by the arm and out of the room; she was panting and crying down a face of chalk.

"What happened? What happened?" I asked.

"I don't know what it was, sir, but we had been walking in the lane and had left the door open. Master Tim was a bit ahead of me and went through the door first, and then he screamed like that."

"Did you see anything that could have frightened him?"

"No, sir, nothing."

I went back to them. It was no good questioning Tim, and there was nothing coherent to be learned from his hysterical sobbing. He grew calmer presently and was taken up to bed. Suddenly he turned to Mary and looked at her with eyes of terror.

"The green monkey—it won't get me, will it, Mummy?"

"No, no, it's all right now," said Mary, and soon after he went to sleep, and then she and I went down to the drawing room. She was on the border of hysteria herself.

"Oh, Tom, what is the matter with this awful house? I'm *terrified*. Ever since I've been here I've been terrified. Do you see things?"

"Yes," I replied.

"Oh, I wish I'd known. I didn't want to worry you if you hadn't. Let me tell you what it's been like. On the day we arrived I saw a man pass ahead of me into my bedroom. Of course, I only *thought* I had. And then I've heard beastly whisperings, and every time I pass that turn in the corridor I *know* there's someone just round the corner. And then the day before you arrived I woke suddenly, and something seemed to force me to go to the window, and I crawled there on hands and knees and peeped through the blind. It was just light enough to see. And suddenly I saw someone running down the lawn, his or her hands outstretched, and there was something ghastly just beside him, and they disappeared behind the trees at the end. I'm terrified every minute."

"What about the servants?"

"Nurse hasn't seen anything, but the others have, I'm certain. And then there are those slimy patches—I think they're the vilest of all. I don't think Tim has been troubled till now, but I'm sure he's been puzzled and uncertain several times."

"Well," I said, "it's pretty obvious we must clear out. I'm seeing Sir William about it tomorrow, I hope, and I'm certain enough of what he'll advise. Meanwhile we must think over where to go. It is a nasty jar, though; I don't mean merely the money, though that's bad enough, but the fuss—just when I hoped we were going to be so happy and settled. However, it's got to be done. We should be mad after a week of this filth-drenched hole."

Just then the telephone bell rang. It was a message to say Sir William would be pleased to see me at half-past ten tomorrow.

With the dusk came that sense of being watched, waited for, followed about, plotted against, an atmosphere of quiet, hunting malignancy. A thick mist came up from the river, and as I was changing for dinner I noticed the lights from the windows seemed to project a series of swiftly changing pictures on its gray, crawling screen. The one opposite my window, for example, was unpleasantly suggestive of three figures staring in and seeming to grow nearer and larger. The effect must have been slightly hypnotic, for suddenly I started back, for it was as if they were about to close on me. I pulled down the blind and hurried downstairs. During dinner we decided that unless Sir William had something very reassuring to say we would go back to London two days later and stay at a hotel till we could find somewhere to spend the next six weeks. Just before going to bed we went up to the night nursery to see if Tim was all right. This room was at the top of a short flight of stairs. As these stairs were covered with green slime, and there was a pool of the muck just outside the door, we took him down to sleep with us.

The Permanent Occupants of The Red Lodge waited till the light was out, but then I felt them come thronging, slipping in one by one, their weapon, fear. It seemed to me they were massed for the attack. A yard away my wife was lying with my son in her arms, so I must fight. I lay back, gripped the sides of the bed, and strove with all my might to hold my assailants back. As the hours went by I felt myself beginning to get the upper hand, and a sense of exaltation came to me. But an hour before dawn they made their greatest effort. I knew that they were willing me to creep on my hands and knees to the window and peep through the blind, and that if I did so we were doomed. As I set my teeth and tightened my grip till I felt racked with agony, the sweat poured from me. I felt them come crowding round the bed and thrusting their faces into mine, and a voice in my head kept saying insistently, "You must crawl to the window and look through the blind." In my mind's eye I could see myself crawling stealthily across the floor and pulling the blind aside, but who would be staring back at me? Just when I felt my resistance breaking I heard a sweet, sleepy twitter from a tree outside, and saw the blind touched by a faint suggestion of light, and at once those with whom I had been struggling left me and went their way, and, utterly exhausted, I slept.

In the morning I found, somewhat ironically, that Mary had slept better than on any night since she came down.

Half-past ten found me entering the Manor House, a delightful, nondescript old place which started wagging its tail as soon as I entered it. Sir William was awaiting me in the library. "I expected this would happen," he said gravely. "And now tell me."

I gave him a short outline of our experiences.

"Yes," he said, "it's always much the same story.

Every time that horrible place has been let I have felt a sense of personal responsibility, and yet I cannot give a proper warning, for the letting of haunted houses is not yet a criminal offense—though it ought to be—and I couldn't afford a libel action, and, as a matter of fact, one old couple had the house for fifteen years and were perfectly delighted with it, being troubled in no way. But now let me tell you what I know of The Red Lodge. I have studied it for forty years, and I regard it as my personal enemy.

"The local tradition is that the second owner, early in the eighteenth century, wished to get rid of his wife and bribed his servants to frighten her to death— just the sort of ancestor I can imagine that blackguard Wilkes being descended from.

"What devilries they perpetrated I don't know, but she is supposed to have rushed from the house just before dawn one day and drowned herself, whereupon her husband installed a small harem in the house. But it was a failure, for each of these charmers one by one rushed down to the river just before dawn, and finally the husband himself did the same. Of the period between then and forty years ago I have no record, but the local tradition has it that it was the scene of tragedy after tragedy and then was shut up for a long time. When I first began to study it, it was occupied by two bachelor brothers. One shot himself in the room which I imagine you use as your bedroom, and the other drowned himself in the usual way. I may tell you that the worst room in the house, the one the unfortunate lady is supposed to have occupied, is locked up—you know, the one on the second floor. I imagine Wilkes mentioned it to you."

"Yes, he did," I replied. "Said he kept important papers there."

"Yes; well, he was forced in self-defense to do so ten years ago, and since then the death rate has been lower, but in those forty years twenty people have taken their lives in the house or in the river, and six children have been drowned accidentally. The last case was Lord Passover's butler in 1924. He was seen to run down to the river and leap in. He was pulled out but had died of shock.

"The people who took the house two years ago left in a week and threatened to bring an action against Wilkes, but they were warned they had no legal case. And I strongly advise you—more than that, *implore* you—to follow their example, though I can imagine the financial loss and great inconvenience, for that house is a deathtrap."

"I will," I replied. "I forgot to mention one thing: When my little boy was so badly frightened he said something about 'a green monkey.'"

"He did!" said Sir William sharply. "Well, then, it is absolutely imperative that you should leave at once. You remember I mentioned the death of certain children. Well, in each case they have been found drowned in the reeds just at the end of that lane, and the people about here have a firm belief that 'The Green Thing,' or 'The Green Death'—it is sometimes referred to as the first and sometimes as the other—is connected with danger to children."

"Have you ever seen anything yourself?" I asked.

"I go to the infernal place as little as possible," replied Sir William, "but when I called on your predecessors I most distinctly saw someone leave the drawing room as we entered it; otherwise, all I have noted is a certain dream which recurs with curious regularity. I find myself standing at the end of the lane and watching the river—always in a sort of brassy half-light. And presently something comes floating down the stream. I can see it jerking up and down, and I always feel passionately anxious to see what it may be. At first I think that it is a log, but when it gets exactly opposite me it changes its course and comes toward me, and then I see that it is a dead body, very decomposed. And when it reaches the bank it begins to climb up toward me, and then, I am thankful to say, I always awake. Sometimes I have thought that one day I shall not wake just then, and that on this occasion something will happen to me, but that is probably merely the silly fancy of an old gentleman who has concerned himself with these singular events rather more than is good for his nerves."

"That is obviously the explanation," I said, "and I am extremely grateful to you. We will leave tomorrow. But don't you think we should attempt to devise some means by which other people may be spared this sort of thing and this brute Wilkes be prevented from letting the house again?"

"I certainly do, and we will discuss it further on

some other occasion. And now go and pack!"

A very great and charming gentleman, Sir William,
I reflected as I walked back to The Red Lodge.

Tim seemed to have recovered excellently well,
but I thought it wise to keep him out of the house
as much as possible, so while Mary and the maids
packed after lunch I went with him for a walk
through the fields. We took our time, and it was only
when the sky grew black and there was a distant
rumble of thunder and a menacing little breeze
came from the west that we turned to come back.
We had to hurry, and as we reached the meadow
next to the house there came a ripping flash and
the storm broke. We started to run for the door into
the garden when I tripped over my bootlace, which
had come undone, and fell. Tim ran on. I had just
tied the lace and was on my feet again when I saw
something slip through the door. It was green, thin,
tall. It seemed to glance back at me, and what should
have been its face was a patch of soused slime. At
that moment Tim saw it, screamed, and ran for the
river. The figure turned and followed him, and before
I could reach him it hovered over him. Tim screamed
again and flung himself in. A moment later I passed
through a green and stenching film and dived
after him. I found him writhing in the reeds and
brought him to the bank. I ran with him in my arms
to the house, and I shall not forget Mary's face as she
saw us from the bedroom window.

By nine o'clock we were all in a hotel in London,
and The Red Lodge was an evil, fading memory. I

shut the front door when I had packed them all into the car. As I took hold of the knob I felt a quick and powerful pressure from the other side, and it shut with a crash. The Permanent Occupants of The Red Lodge were in sole possession once more.

Sredni Vashtar

Saki

CONRADIN WAS TEN years old, and the doctor had pronounced his professional opinion that the boy would not live another five years. The doctor was silky and effete and counted for little, but his opinion was endorsed by Mrs. De Ropp, who counted for nearly everything. Mrs. De Ropp was Conradin's cousin and guardian, and in his eyes she represented those three-fifths of the world that are necessary and disagreeable and real; the other two-fifths, in perpetual antagonism to the foregoing, were summed up in himself and his imagination. One of these days Conradin supposed he would succumb to the mastering pressure of wearisome necessary things—such as illnesses and coddling restrictions and drawn-out dullness. Without his imagination, which was rampant under the spur of loneliness, he would have succumbed long ago.

Mrs. De Ropp would never, in her honestest moments, have confessed to herself that she disliked Conradin, though she might have been dimly aware that thwarting him "for his good" was a duty which she did not find particularly irksome. Conradin hated her with a desperate sincerity which he was perfectly able to mask. Such few pleasures as he could contrive for himself gained an added relish from the likelihood that they would be displeasing to his guardian, and from the realm of his imagination she was locked out—an unclean thing, which should find no entrance.

In the dull, cheerless garden, overlooked by so many windows that were ready to open with a message not to do this or that or a reminder that medicines were due, he found little attraction. The few fruit trees that it contained were set jealously apart from his plucking, as though they were rare specimens of their kind blooming in an arid waste; it would probably have been difficult to find a market-gardener who would have offered ten shillings for their entire yearly produce. In a forgotten corner, however, almost hidden behind a dismal shrubbery, was a disused tool shed of respectable proportions, and within its walls Conradin found a haven, something that took on the varying aspects of a playroom and a cathedral. He had peopled it with a legion of familiar phantoms, evoked partly from fragments of history and partly from his own brain, but it also boasted two inmates of flesh and blood. In one corner lived a ragged-plumaged Houdan hen, on which the boy lavished an affection that had scarcely another outlet. Farther back in the gloom stood a large hutch, divided into two compartments, one of which was fronted with close iron bars. This was the abode of a large polecat-ferret, which a friendly butcher boy had once smuggled, cage and all, into its present quarters, in exchange for a long-secreted hoard of small silver. Conradin was dreadfully afraid of the lithe, sharp-fanged beast, but it was his most treasured possession. Its very presence in the tool shed was a secret and fearful joy, to be kept scrupulously from the knowledge of the Woman, as he privately dubbed his cousin. And one day, out of heaven knows what material, he spun the beast a wonderful name, and from that moment it grew into a god and a religion. The Woman indulged in religion once a week at a church nearby and took Conradin with her, but to him the church service was an alien rite in the House of Rimmon. Every Thursday, in the dim and musty silence of the tool shed, he worshipped with mystic and elaborate ceremonial before the wooden hutch where dwelt Sredni Vashtar, the great ferret. Red flowers in their season and scarlet berries in the wintertime were offered at his shrine, for he was a god who laid some special stress on the fierce, impatient side of things, as opposed to the Woman's religion, which, as far as Conradin could observe, went to great lengths in the contrary direction. And on great festivals powdered nutmeg was strewn in front of his hutch, an important feature of the offering being that the nutmeg had to be stolen. These festivals were of irregular occurrence and were chiefly appointed to celebrate some passing event. On one occasion, when Mrs. De Ropp suffered from acute toothache for three days, Conradin kept up the festival during the entire three days and almost succeeded in persuading himself that Sredni Vashtar was personally responsible for the toothache. If the malady had lasted for another day the supply of nutmeg would have given out.

The Houdan hen was never drawn into the cult of Sredni Vashtar. Conradin had long ago settled that she was Anabaptist. He did not pretend to have the remotest knowledge as to what an Anabaptist was, but he privately hoped that it was dashing and not very respectable. Mrs. De Ropp was the ground plan on which he based and detested all respectability.

After a while Conradin's absorption in the tool shed began to attract the notice of his guardian. "It is not good for him to be pottering down there in all weather," she promptly decided, and at breakfast one morning she announced that the Houdan hen had been sold and taken away overnight. With her shortsighted eyes she peered at Conradin, waiting for an outbreak of rage and sorrow, which she was ready to rebuke with a flow of excellent precepts and reasoning. But Conradin said nothing: there was nothing to be said. Something perhaps in his white, set face gave her a momentary qualm, for at tea that afternoon there was toast on the table, a delicacy which she usually banned on the ground that it was bad for him—also because the making of it "gave trouble," a deadly offense in the middle-class feminine eye.

"I thought you liked toast," she exclaimed with an injured air, observing that he did not touch it.

"Sometimes," said Conradin.

In the shed that evening there was an innovation in the worship of the hutch-god. Conradin had been wont to chant his praises; tonight he asked a boon.

"Do one thing for me, Sredni Vashtar."

The thing was not specified. As Sredni Vashtar was a god, he must be supposed to know. And choking back a sob as he looked at that other empty corner, Conradin went back to the world he so hated.

And every night, in the welcome darkness of his bedroom, and every evening in the dusk of the tool shed, Conradin's bitter litany went up: "Do one thing for me, Sredni Vashtar."

Mrs. De Ropp noticed that the visits to the shed did not cease, and one day she made a further journey of inspection.

"What are you keeping in that locked hutch?" she asked. "I believe it's guinea pigs. I'll have them all cleared away."

Conradin shut his lips tight, but the Woman ransacked his bedroom till she found the carefully hidden key and forthwith marched down to the shed to complete her discovery. It was a cold afternoon, and Conradin had been bidden to keep to the house. From the farthest window of the dining room the door of the shed could just be seen beyond the corner of the shrubbery, and there Conradin stationed himself. He saw the Woman enter, and then he imagined her opening the door of the sacred hutch and peering down with her shortsighted eyes into the thick straw bed where his god lay hidden. Perhaps she would prod at the straw in her clumsy impatience. And

Conradin fervently breathed his prayer for the last time. But he knew as he prayed that he did not believe. He knew that the Woman would come out presently with that pursed smile he loathed so well on her face, and that in an hour or two the gardener would carry away his wonderful god, a god no longer, but a simple brown ferret in a hutch. And he knew that the Woman would triumph always as she triumphed now, and that he would grow ever more sickly under her pestering and domineering and superior wisdom, till one day nothing would matter much more with him, and the doctor would be proved right. And in the sting and misery of his defeat, he began to chant loudly and defiantly the hymn of his threatened idol:

"Sredni Vashtar went forth;
His thoughts were red thoughts and his teeth were white.
His enemies called for peace, but he brought them death.
Sredni Vashtar the Beautiful."

And then of a sudden he stopped his chanting and drew closer to the windowpane. The door of the shed still stood ajar as it had been left, and the minutes were slipping by. They were long minutes, but they slipped by nevertheless. He watched the starlings running and flying in little parties across the lawn; he counted them over and over again, with one eye always on that swinging door. A sour-faced maid came in to lay the table for tea, and still Conradin stood and waited and watched. Hope had crept

by inches into his heart, and now a look of triumph
began to blaze in his eyes that had only known the
wistful patience of defeat. Under his breath, with a
furtive exultation, he began once again the paean of
victory and devastation. And presently his eyes were
rewarded: out through that doorway came a long,
low, yellow and brown beast, with eyes a-blink at
the waning daylight and dark wet stains around the
fur of jaws and throat. Conradin dropped on his
knees. The great polecat-ferret made its way down
to a small brook at the foot of the garden, drank for
a moment, then crossed a little plank bridge and was
lost to sight in the bushes. Such was the passing of
Sredni Vashtar.

"Tea is ready," said the sour-faced maid. "Where
is the mistress?"

"She went down to the shed some time ago," said
Conradin.

And while the maid went to summon her mistress
to tea, Conradin fished a toasting fork out of the
sideboard drawer and proceeded to toast himself a
piece of bread. And during the toasting of it and the
buttering of it with much butter and the slow enjoyment of eating it, Conradin listened to the noises and
silences which fell in quick spasms beyond the dining-
room door. The loud, foolish screaming of the maid,
the answering chorus of wondering ejaculations from
the kitchen region, the scuttering footsteps and hurried embassies for outside help, and then, after a
lull, the scared sobbings and the shuffling tread of
those who bore a heavy burden into the house.

"Whoever will break it to the poor child? I couldn't for the life of me!" exclaimed a shrill voice. And while they debated the matter among themselves, Conradin made himself another piece of toast.

Thurnley Abbey

Perceval Landon

THREE YEARS AGO I was on my way out to the East, and as an extra day in London was of some importance I took the Friday evening mail train to Brindisi instead of the usual Thursday morning Marseilles Express. Many people shrink from the long forty-eight-hour train journey through Europe and the subsequent rush across the Mediterranean on the nineteen-knot *Isis* or *Osiris;* but there is really very little discomfort on either the train or the mail boat, and, unless there is actually nothing for me to do, I always like to save the extra day and a half in London before I say good-bye to her for one of my longer tramps.

This time—it was early, I remember, in the shipping season, probably about the beginning of September—there were few passengers, and I had a compartment in the P. & O. Indian Express to myself all the way from Calais. All Sunday I watched the blue waves dimpling the Adriatic and the pale rosemary along the cuttings; the plain, white towns, with their flat roofs and their bold *duomos;* and the gray-green, gnarled olive orchards of Apulia. The journey was just like any other. We ate in the dining car as often and as long as we decently could. We slept after luncheon; we dawdled the afternoon away with yellow-backed novels; sometimes we exchanged platitudes in the smoking room, and it was there that I met Alastair Colvin.

Colvin was a man of middle height, with a resolute, well-cut jaw; his hair was turning gray; his moustache was sun-whitened; otherwise he was clean-shaven— obviously a gentleman, and obviously also a preoccupied man. He had no great wit. When spoken to, he made the usual remarks in the right way, and I daresay he refrained from banalities only because he spoke less than the rest of us; most of the time he buried himself in the Wagon-lit Company's timetable, but seemed unable to concentrate his attention on any one page of it. He found that I had been over the Siberian Railway, and for a quarter of an hour he discussed it with me. Then he lost interest in it and rose to go to his compartment. But he came back again very soon and seemed glad to pick up the conversation again.

Of course this did not seem to me to be of any importance. Most travelers by train become a trifle infirm of purpose after thirty-six hours' rattling. But Colvin's restless way I noticed in somewhat marked contrast with the man's personal importance and dignity; especially ill-suited was it to his finely made, large hand, with its strong, broad, regular nails and its few lines. As I looked at his hand I noticed a long, deep, and recent scar of ragged shape. However, it

is absurd to pretend that I thought anything was
unusual. I went off at five o'clock on Sunday afternoon to sleep away the hour or two that had still to
be got through before we arrived at Brindisi.

Once there, we few passengers transshipped our
hand baggage, verified our berths—there were only a
score of us in all—and then, after an aimless ramble
of half an hour in Brindisi, we returned to dinner at
the Hotel International, not wholly surprised that the
town had been the death of Virgil. If I remember
rightly, there is a gaily painted hall at the International—I do not wish to advertise anything, but there
is no other place in Brindisi at which to await the
coming of the mails—and after dinner I was looking
with awe at a trellis overgrown with blue vines, when
Colvin moved across the room to my table. He picked
up *Il Secolo* but almost immediately gave up the
pretense of reading it. He turned squarely to me and
said, "Would you do me a favor?"

One doesn't do favors to stray acquaintances on
Continental expresses without knowing something
more of them than I knew of Colvin. But I smiled in
a noncommittal way and asked him what he wanted.
I wasn't wrong in part of my estimate of him; he said
bluntly, "Will you let me sleep in your cabin on the
Osiris?" And he colored a little as he said it.

Now, there is nothing more tiresome than having
to put up with a stable-companion at sea, and I
asked him rather pointedly, "Surely there is room for
all of us?" I thought that perhaps he had been part-
nered off with some mangy Levantine and wanted to

escape from him at all hazards.

Colvin, still somewhat confused, said, "Yes, I am in a cabin by myself. But you would do me the greatest favor if you would allow me to share yours."

This was all very well, but, besides the fact that I always sleep better when alone, there had been some recent thefts on board English liners, and I hesitated, frank and honest and self-conscious as Colvin was. Just then the mail train came in with a clatter and a rush of escaping steam, and I asked him to see me again about it on the boat when we started. He answered me curtly—I suppose he saw the mistrust in my manner—"I am a member of White's." I smiled to myself as he said it, but I remembered in a moment that the man—if he were really what he claimed to be, and I make no doubt that he was—must have been sorely put to it before he urged the fact as a guarantee of his respectability to a total stranger at a Brindisi hotel.

That evening, as we cleared the red and green harbor lights of Brindisi, Colvin explained. This is his story in his own words.

"When I was traveling in India some years ago, I made the acquaintance of a youngish man in the woods and forests. We camped out together for a week, and I found him a pleasant companion. John Broughton was a lighthearted soul when off duty, but a steady and capable man in any of the small emergencies that continually arise in that department. He was liked and trusted by the natives, and,

though a trifle over-pleased with himself when he
escaped to civilization at Simla or Calcutta, Broughton's future was well assured in government service
when a fair-sized estate was unexpectedly left to
him, and he joyfully shook the dust of the Indian
plains from his feet and returned to England.

"For five years he drifted about London. I saw
him now and then. We dined together about every
eighteen months, and I could trace pretty exactly
the gradual sickening of Broughton with a merely
idle life. He then set out on a couple of long voyages,
returned as restless as before, and at last told me that
he had decided to marry and settle down at his
place, Thurnley Abbey, which had long been empty.
He spoke about looking after the property and standing for his constituency in the usual way. Vivien
Wilde, his fiancée, had, I suppose, begun to take him
in hand. She was a pretty girl with a deal of fair hair
and rather an exclusive manner; deeply religious in
a narrow school, she was still kindly and high-
spirited, and I thought that Broughton was in luck.
He was quite happy and full of information about his
future.

"Among other things, I asked him about Thurnley
Abbey. He confessed that he hardly knew the place.
The last tenant, a man called Clarke, had lived in
one wing for fifteen years and seen no one. He had
been a miser and a hermit. It was the rarest thing for
a light to be seen at the Abbey after dark. Only the
barest necessities of life were ordered, and the tenant himself received them at the side door. His one

half-caste manservant, after a month's stay in the house, had abruptly left without warning and had returned to the Southern States.

"One thing Broughton complained bitterly about: Clarke had willfully spread the rumor among the villagers that the Abbey was haunted and had even condescended to play childish tricks with spirit lamps and salt in order to scare trespassers away at night. He had been detected in the act of this tomfoolery, but the story spread, and no one, said Broughton, would venture near the house, except in broad daylight. The hauntedness of Thurnley Abbey was now, he said with a grin, part of the gospel of the countryside, but he and his young wife were going to change all that. Would I propose myself any time I liked? I, of course, said I would, and equally, of course, intended to do nothing of the sort without a definite invitation.

"The house was put in thorough repair, though not a stick of the old furniture and tapestry was removed. Floors and ceilings were relaid, the roof was made watertight again, and the dust of half a century was scoured out. He showed me some photographs of the place. It was called an abbey, though as a matter of fact it had been only the infirmary of the long-vanished Abbey of Closter, some five miles away. The larger part of this building remained as it had been in pre-Reformation days, but a wing had been added in Jacobean times, and that part of the house had been kept in something like repair by Mr. Clarke. He had in both the ground and first floors set a heavy timber door, strongly barred with iron, in the passage between the earlier and the Jacobean parts of the house and had entirely neglected the former. So there had been a good deal of work to be done.

"Broughton, whom I saw in London two or three times about this period, made a deal of fun over the positive refusal of the workmen to remain after sundown. Even after the electric light had been put into every room, nothing would induce them to remain, though, as Broughton observed, electric light was death on ghosts. The legend of the Abbey's ghosts had gone far and wide, and the men would take no risks. They went home in batches of five and six, and even during the daylight hours there was an inordinate amount of talking between one and another, if either happened to be out of sight of his companion. On the whole, though nothing of any sort or kind had been conjured up even by their heated imaginations during their five months' work upon the Abbey, the belief in the ghosts was rather strengthened than otherwise in Thurnley because of the men's confessed nervousness, and local tradition declared itself in favor of the ghost of an immured nun.

" 'Good old nun!' said Broughton.

"I asked him whether in general he believed in the possibility of ghosts, and, rather to my surprise, he said that he couldn't say he entirely disbelieved in them. A man in India had told him one morning in camp that he believed that his mother was dead in England, as her vision had come to his tent the night before. He had not been alarmed but had said nothing, and the figure vanished again. As a matter of fact, the next possible *dak-walla* brought a telegram announcing the mother's death. 'There the thing was,' said Broughton. But at Thurnley he was practical enough. He roundly cursed the idiotic selfishness of Clarke, whose silly antics had caused all the inconvenience. At the same time, he couldn't refuse to sympathize to some extent with the ignorant workmen. 'My own idea,' said he, 'is that if a ghost ever does come in one's way, one ought to speak to it.'

"I agreed. Little as I knew of the ghost world and its conventions, I had always remembered that a spook was in honor bound to wait to be spoken to. It didn't seem much to do, and I felt that the sound of one's own voice would at any rate reassure oneself as to one's wakefulness. But there are few ghosts outside Europe—few, that is, that a white man can see—and I had never been troubled with any. However, as I have said, I told Broughton that I agreed.

"So the wedding took place, and I went to it in a tall hat which I bought for the occasion, and the new Mrs. Broughton smiled very nicely at me afterward. As it had to happen, I took the Orient Express that evening and was not in England again for nearly six months. Just before I came back I got a letter from Broughton. He asked if I could see him in London or come to Thurnley, as he thought I should be better able to help him than anyone else he knew. His wife sent a nice message to me at the end, so I was reassured about at least one thing. I wrote from

Budapest that I would come and see him at Thurnley two days after my arrival in London, and as I sauntered out of the Pannonia into the Kerepesi Utcza to post my letters I wondered of what earthly service I could be to Broughton. I had been out with him after tiger on foot, and I could imagine few men better able at a pinch to manage their own business. However, I had nothing to do, so after dealing with some small accumulations of business during my absence I packed a kit bag and departed to Euston.

"I was met by Broughton's great limousine at Thurnley Road station, and after a drive of nearly seven miles we echoed through the sleepy streets of Thurnley Village, into which the main gates of the park thrust themselves, splendid with pillars and spread eagles and tomcats rampant atop of them. I never was a herald, but I know that the Broughtons have the right to supporters—heaven knows why! From the gates a quadruple avenue of beech trees led inward for a quarter of a mile. Beneath them a neat strip of fine turf edged the road and ran back until the poison of the dead beech leaves killed it under the trees. There were many wheel tracks on the road, and a comfortable little pony trap jogged past me laden with a country parson and his wife and daughter. Evidently there was some garden party going on at the Abbey. The road dropped away to the right at the end of the avenue, and I could see the Abbey across a wide pasturage and a broad lawn thickly dotted with guests.

"The end of the building was plain. It must have

been almost mercilessly austere when it was first built, but time had crumbled the edges and toned the stone down to an orange-lichened gray wherever it showed behind its curtain of magnolia, jasmine, and ivy. Farther on was the three-storied Jacobean house, tall and handsome. There had not been the slightest attempt to adapt the one to the other, but the kindly ivy had glossed over the touching point. There was a tall flèche in the middle of the building, surmounting a small bell tower. Behind the house there rose the mountainous verdure of Spanish chestnuts all the way up the hill.

"Broughton had seen me coming from afar and walked across from his other guests to welcome me before turning me over to the butler's care. This man was sandy-haired and rather inclined to be talkative. He could, however, answer hardly any questions about the house; he had, he said, been there only three weeks. Mindful of what Broughton had told me, I made no inquiries about ghosts, though the room into which I was shown might have justified anything. It was a very large, low room with oak beams projecting from the white ceiling. Every inch of the walls, including the doors, was covered with tapestry, and a remarkably fine Italian four-post bedstead, heavily draped, added to the darkness and dignity of the place. All the furniture was old, well made, and dark. Underfoot there was a plain green pile carpet, the only new thing about the room except the electric light fittings and the jugs and basins. Even the looking glass on the dressing table was an old pyramidal Venetian glass set in heavy *repoussé* frame of tarnished silver.

"After a few minutes' cleaning up, I went downstairs and out upon the lawn, where I greeted my hostess. The people gathered there were of the usual country type, all anxious to be pleased and roundly curious as to the new master of the Abbey. Rather to my surprise and quite to my pleasure, I rediscovered Glenham, whom I had known well in old days in Barotseland; he lived quite close, as, he remarked with a grin, I ought to have known. 'But,' he added, 'I don't live in a place like this.' He swept his hand to the long, low lines of the Abbey in obvious admiration, and then, to my intense interest, muttered beneath his breath, 'Thank God!' He saw that I had overheard him, and turning to me said decidedly, 'Yes, "Thank God" I said, and I meant it. I wouldn't live at the Abbey for all Broughton's money.'

" 'But surely,' I demurred, 'you know that old Clarke was discovered in the very act of setting light to his bugaboos.'

"Glenham shrugged his shoulders. 'Yes, I know about that. But there is something wrong with the place still. All I can say is that Broughton is a different man since he has lived here. I don't believe that he will remain much longer. But—you're staying here? Well, you'll hear all about it tonight. There's a big dinner, I understand.' The conversation turned off to old reminiscences, and Glenham soon after had to go.

"Before I went to dress that evening I had twenty minutes' talk with Broughton in his library. There was no doubt that the man was altered—gravely altered. He was nervous and fidgety, and I found him looking at me only when my eye was off him. I naturally asked him what he wanted of me. I told him I would do anything I could, but that I couldn't conceive what he lacked that I could provide. He said with a lusterless smile that there was, however, something, and that he would tell me the following morning. It struck me that he was somehow ashamed of himself, and perhaps ashamed of the part he was asking me to play. However, I dismissed the subject from my mind and went up to dress in my palatial room. As I shut the door a draft blew out the Queen of Sheba from the wall, and I noticed that the tapestries were not fastened to the wall at the bottom. I have always held very practical views about spooks, and it has often seemed to me that the slow waving in firelight of loose tapestry upon a wall would account for ninety-nine percent of the stories one hears. Certainly the dignified undulation of this lady with her attendants and huntsmen—one of whom was untidily cutting the throat of a fallow deer upon the very steps on which King Solomon, a gray-faced Flemish nobleman with the order of the Golden Fleece, awaited his fair visitor—gave color to my hypothesis.

"Nothing much happened at dinner. The people were very much like those of the garden party. A young woman next to me seemed anxious to know what was being read in London. As she was far more familiar than I with the most recent magazines and

literary supplements, I found salvation in being myself instructed in the tendencies of modern fiction.
All true art, she said, was shot through and through
with melancholy. How vulgar were the attempts at
wit that marked so many modern books! From the
beginning of literature it had always been tragedy
that embodied the highest attainment of every age.
To call such works morbid merely begged the question. No thoughtful man—she looked sternly at me
through the steel rim of her glasses—could fail to
agree with her.

"Of course, as one would, I immediately and prop-
erly said that I slept with Pett Ridge and Jacobs
under my pillow at night, and that if *Jorrocks* weren't
quite so large and cornery, I would add him to the
company. She hadn't read any of them, so I was
saved—for a time. But I remember grimly that she
said that the dearest wish of her life was to be in
some awful and soul-freezing situation of horror,
and I remember that she dealt hardly with the hero
of Nat Paynter's vampire story between nibbles at
her brown-bread ice. She was a cheerless soul, and
I couldn't help thinking that if there were many such
in the neighborhood it was not surprising that old
Glenham had been stuffed with some nonsense or
other about the Abbey. Yet nothing could well have
been less creepy than the glitter of silver and glass
and the subdued lights and cackle of conversation
all round the dinner table.

"After the ladies had gone I found myself talking
to the rural dean. He was a thin, earnest man who

at once turned the conversation to old Clarke's buf-
fooneries. But, he said, Mr. Broughton had intro-
duced such a new and cheerful spirit, not only into
the Abbey but, he might say, into the whole neighborhood, that he had great hopes that the ignorant
superstitions of the past were from henceforth des-
tined to oblivion. Thereupon his other neighbor, a
portly gentleman of independent means and position,
audibly remarked 'Amen,' which damped the rural
dean, and we talked of partridges past, partridges
present, and pheasants to come. At the other end of
the table Broughton sat with a couple of his friends,
red-faced hunting men. Once I noticed that they
were discussing me, but I paid no attention to it at
the time. I remembered it a few hours later.

"By eleven all the guests were gone, and Broughton, his wife, and I were alone together under the
fine plaster ceiling of the Jacobean drawing room.
Mrs. Broughton talked about one or two of the
neighbors and then, with a smile, said that she knew
I would excuse her, shook hands with me, and went
off to bed. I am not very good at analyzing things,
but I felt that she talked a little uncomfortably and
with a suspicion of effort, smiled rather conven-
tionally, and was obviously glad to go. These things
seem trifling enough to repeat, but I had throughout
the faint feeling that everything was not square.
Under the circumstances, this was enough to set me
wondering what on earth the service could be that
I was to render—wondering also whether the whole
business were not some ill-advised jest in order to

make me come down from London for a mere shooting party.

"Broughton said little after she had gone. But he was evidently laboring to bring the conversation round to the so-called haunting of the Abbey. As soon as I saw this, of course, I asked him directly about it. He then seemed at once to lose interest in the matter. There was no doubt about it: Broughton was somehow a changed man, and to my mind he had changed in no way for the better. Mrs. Boughton seemed no sufficient cause. He was clearly very fond of her and she of him. I reminded him that he was going to tell me what I could do for him in the morning, pleaded my journey, lighted a candle, and went upstairs with him. At the end of the passage leading into the old house he grinned weakly and said, 'Mind, if you see a ghost, do talk to it; you said you would.' He stood irresolutely a moment and then turned away. At the door of his dressing room he paused once more. 'I'm here,' he called out, 'if you should want anything. Good night.' And he shut his door.

"I went along the passage to my room, undressed, switched on a lamp beside my bed, read a few pages of *The Jungle Book*, and then, more than ready for sleep, turned the light off and went fast asleep.

"Three hours later I woke up. There was not a breath of wind outside. There was not even a flicker of light from the fireplace. As I lay there, an ash tinkled slightly as it cooled, but there was hardly a gleam of the dullest red in the grate. An owl cried among the silent Spanish chestnuts on the slope outside. I idly reviewed the events of the day, hoping that I should fall off to sleep again before I reached dinner. But at the end I seemed as wakeful as ever. There was no help for it. I must read my *Jungle Book* again till I felt ready to go off, so I fumbled for the pear at the end of the cord that hung down inside the bed, and I switched on the bedside lamp. The sudden glory dazzled me for a moment. I felt under my pillow for my book with half-shut eyes. Then, growing used to the light, I happened to look down to the foot of my bed.

"I can never tell you really what happened then. Nothing I could ever confess in the most abject words could even faintly picture to you what I felt. I know that my heart stopped dead, and my throat shut automatically. In one instinctive movement I crouched back up against the headboards of the bed, staring at the horror. The movement set my heart going again, and the sweat dripped from every pore. I am not a particularly religious man, but I had always believed that God would never allow any supernatural appearance to present itself to man in such a guise and in such circumstances that harm, either bodily or mental, could result to him. I can only tell you that at that moment both my life and my reason rocked unsteadily on their seats."

The other *Osiris* passengers had gone to bed. Only he and I remained leaning over the starboard railing,

which rattled uneasily now and then under the fierce vibration of the over-engined mail boat. Far over, there were the lights of a few fishing smacks riding out the night, and a great rush of white combing and seething water fell out and away from us overside.

At last Colvin went on:

"Leaning over the foot of my bed, looking at me, was a figure swathed in a rotten and tattered veiling. This shroud passed over the head, but left both eyes and the right side of the face bare. It then followed the line of the arm down to where the hand grasped the bed end. The face was not entirely that of a skull, though the eyes and the flesh of the face were totally gone. There was a thin, dry skin drawn tightly over the features, and there was some skin left on the hand. One wisp of hair crossed the forehead. It was perfectly still. I looked at it, and it looked at me, and my brains turned dry and hot in my head. I had still got the pear of the electric lamp in my hand, and I played idly with it; only I dared not turn the light out again. I shut my eyes only to open them in a hideous terror the same second. The thing had not moved. My heart was thumping, and the sweat cooled me as it evaporated. Another cinder tinkled in the grate, and a panel creaked in the wall.

"My reason failed me. For twenty minutes, or twenty seconds, I was able to think of nothing else but this awful figure, till there came, hurtling through the empty channels of my senses, the remembrance that Broughton and his friends had discussed me furtively at dinner. The dim possibility of its being a hoax stole gratefully into my unhappy mind, and once there, my pluck came creeping back along a thousand tiny veins. My first sensation was one of blind, unreasoning thankfulness that my brain was going to stand the trial. I am not a timid man, but the best of us needs some human handle to steady him in time of extremity, and in this faint but growing hope that after all it might be only a brutal hoax, I found the fulcrum that I needed. At last I moved.

"How I managed to do it I cannot tell you, but with one spring toward the foot of the bed I got within arm's length and struck one fearful blow with my fist at the thing. It crumbled under it, and my hand was cut to the bone. With a sickening revulsion after my terror, I dropped, half-fainting, across the end of the bed. So it was merely a foul trick after all. No doubt the trick had been played many a time before; no doubt Broughton and his friends had had some large bet among themselves as to what I should do when I discovered the gruesome thing. From my state of abject terror I found myself transported into an insensate anger. I shouted curses upon Broughton. I dived rather than climbed over the bed end onto the sofa. I tore at the robed skeleton—how well the whole thing had been carried out, I thought—I broke the skull against the floor and stamped upon its dry bones. I flung the head away under the bed and rent the brittle bones of the trunk in pieces. I snapped the thin thighbones across my knee and flung them in different directions. The shinbones I set up against a stool and broke with my heel. I raged like a berserker against the loathly thing and stripped the ribs from the backbone and slung the breastbone against the cupboard. My fury increased as the work of destruction went on. I tore the frail, rotten veil into twenty pieces, and the dust went up over everything, over the clean blotting paper and the silver inkstand.

"At last my work was done. There was but a raffle of broken bones and strips of parchment and crumbling wool. Then, picking up a piece of the skull—it was the cheek and temple bone of the right side, I remember—I opened the door and went down the passage to Broughton's dressing room. I remember still how my sweat-dripping pajamas clung to me as I walked. At the door, I kicked and entered.

"Broughton was in bed. He had already turned the light on and seemed shrunken and horrified. For a moment he could hardly pull himself together. Then I spoke. I don't know what I said. I only know that from a heart full and overfull with hatred and contempt, spurred on by shame of my own recent cowardice, I let my tongue run on. He answered nothing. I was amazed at my own fluency. My hair still clung lankily to my wet temples, my hand was bleeding profusely, and I must have looked a strange sight. Broughton huddled himself up at the head of the bed just as I had. Still he made no answer, no defense. He seemed preoccupied with something beside my reproaches and once or twice moistened his lips with his tongue. But he could say nothing, though he moved his hands now and then, just as a baby who cannot speak moves its hands.

"At last the door into Mrs. Broughton's room opened and she came in, white and terrified. 'What is it? What is it? Oh, in God's name, what is it?' she cried again and again, and then she went up to her husband and sat on the bed in her nightdress, and the two faced me. I told her what the matter was. I spared her husband not a word for her presence there. Yet he seemed hardly to understand. I told the pair that I had spoiled their cowardly joke for them. Broughton looked up.

" 'I have smashed the foul thing into a hundred pieces,' I said. Broughton licked his lips again and his mouth worked. 'By God,' I shouted, 'it would serve you right if I thrashed you within an inch of your life. I will take care that no decent man or woman of my acquaintance ever speaks to you again. And there—' I added, throwing the broken piece of the skull upon the floor beside his bed, 'there is a souvenir for you of your damned work tonight!'

"Broughton saw the bone, and in a moment it was his turn to frighten me. He squealed like a hare caught in a trap. He screamed and screamed till Mrs. Broughton, almost as bewildered as myself, held on to him and coaxed him like a child to be quiet. But Broughton—and as he moved I thought that ten minutes ago I perhaps looked as terribly ill as he did—thrust her from him and scrambled out of the bed onto the floor and, still screaming, put out his hand to the bone. It had blood on it from my hand. He paid no attention to me whatever. In truth, I said nothing. This was a new turn indeed to the horrors of the evening. He rose from the floor with the bone in his hand and stood silent. He seemed to be listening. 'Time, time, perhaps,' he muttered and almost at the same moment fell at full length on the carpet, cutting his head against the fender. The bone flew from his hand and came to rest near the door. I picked Broughton up, haggard and broken, with blood over his face. He whispered hoarsely and quickly, 'Listen, listen!' We listened.

"After ten seconds' utter quiet, I seemed to hear something. I could not be sure, but at last there was no doubt. There was a quiet sound as of one moving along the passage. Little regular steps came toward us over the hard oak flooring. Broughton moved to where his wife sat white and speechless on the bed and pressed her face into his shoulder.

"Then, the last thing I could see as he turned the light out, he fell forward with his own head pressed into the pillow of the bed. Something in their company, something in their cowardice, helped me, and I faced the open doorway of the room which was outlined fairly clearly against the dimly lighted passage. I put out one hand and touched Mrs. Broughton's shoulder in the darkness. But at the last moment I, too, failed. I sank on my knees and put my face in the bed. Only we all heard. The footsteps came to the door, and there they stopped. The piece of bone was lying a yard inside the door. There was a rustle of moving stuff, and the thing was in the room. Mrs. Broughton was silent; I could hear Broughton's voice praying, muffled in the pillow; I was cursing my own cowardice. Then the steps moved out again on the oak boards of the passage, and I heard the sounds dying away. In a flash of remorse I went to the door and looked out. At the end of the corridor I thought I saw something that moved away. A moment later the passage was empty. I stood with my forehead against the jamb of the door almost physically sick.

" 'You can turn the light on,' I said, and there was an answering flare. There was no bone at my feet. Mrs. Broughton had fainted. Broughton was almost useless, and it took me ten minutes to bring her to. Broughton only said one thing worth remembering. For the most part he went on muttering prayers. But I was glad afterward to recollect that he had said that thing. He said in a colorless voice, half as a question, half as a reproach, 'You didn't speak to her.'

"We spent the remainder of the night together. Mrs. Broughton actually fell off into a kind of sleep before dawn, but she suffered so horribly in her dreams that I shook her into consciousness again. Never was dawn so long in coming. Three or four times Broughton spoke to himself. Mrs. Broughton would then just tighten her hold on his arm, but she could say nothing. As for me, I can honestly say that I grew worse as the hours passed and the light strengthened. The two violent reactions had battered down my steadiness of view, and I felt that the foundations of my life had been built upon the sand. I said nothing, and after binding up my hand with a towel I did not move. It was better so. They helped me and I helped them, and we all three knew that our reason had gone very near to ruin that night.

"At last, when the light came in pretty strongly and the birds outside were chattering and singing, we felt that we must do something. Yet we never moved. You might have thought that we should particularly dislike being found as we were by the servants—yet nothing of that kind mattered a straw, and an over-powering listlessness found us as we sat, until Chapman, Broughton's man, actually knocked and opened the door. None of us moved. Broughton, speaking hardly and stiffly, said, 'Chapman, you can come back in five minutes.' Chapman was a discreet man, but it would have made no difference to us if he had carried his news to the 'room' at once.

"We looked at one another and I said I must go back. I meant to wait outside until Chapman returned. I simply dared not reenter my bedroom alone. Broughton roused himself and said that he would come with me. Mrs. Broughton agreed to remain in her own room for five minutes if the blinds were drawn up and all the doors left open.

"So Broughton and I, leaning stiffly one against the other, went down to my room. By the morning light that filtered past the blinds we could see our way, and I released the blinds. There was nothing wrong in the room from end to end except smears of my own blood on the end of the bed, on the sofa, and on the carpet where I had torn the thing to pieces."

Colvin had finished his story. There was nothing to say. Seven bells stuttered out from the forecastle, and the answering cry wailed through the darkness. I took him downstairs.

"Of course, I am much better now, but it is a kindness of you to let me sleep in your cabin."

"God Grante That She Lye Stille"

Cynthia Asquith

It was not until three weeks after I came to live at
Mosstone that I first saw her, but most of my new
patients had talked to me of Margaret Clewer, the
youthful owner of the Manor House. Many shook
kindly heads because she was so alone in the world.
"Only twenty-two and without a single near relation!"
But they also spoke of her beauty and charm, and it
was with agreeable curiosity that I set out to pay my
professional call at what the Mosstone villagers called
the great house.

As I passed through the gateway that I had so
often admired from outside into a large, gray-walled
court, the muffled atmosphere of the place seemed to
envelop me like a cloak. The very air seemed thicker
and more still. It was as though I had stepped out
of the everyday world into something cloistered and
self-sufficing. Pigeons fluttered and crooned, and
plumes of blue smoke rose into the golden air. Ab-
sorbing its beauty like a long, lovely draft, I gazed
at the exquisite gabled house, with its great mullioned
windows and queer twisted chimneys, around which
the swallows skimmed. It struck me then, I remem-

ber, that more than any other building I had ever
seen, this house appeared to have a face, an actual
countenance that might vary like that of a beautiful
woman. Yet could any building look more remote,
more strikingly aloof? Time had deposited so much
on those mellowed walls; for so many centuries a
deep reservoir of life, the house now looked with-
drawn from any further participation, as though with
gentle repudiation dissociating itself from the present and the future.

My watch told me I had returned from my walk
twenty minutes before I was due. Ever since my boy-
hood I had loved poring over old epitaphs, so I
turned into the churchyard, which was only a few
yards from the front windows of the house.

Like most village churchyards it was very over-
crowded, but the dark, red-fruited yew trees shed
an air of somber peace over the clustered graves.
Most of these graves were mere uncommemorated
grass mounds, but there were also a number of gray
lichen-clad tombstones lying and leaning at all
angles, and on many of these the name of Clewer
was engraved. Evidently innumerable generations
of my future patient's family had lived and died
here. Most of these long-dead Clewers seemed to
have been mourned by appreciative and verbose
relations. Nothing that uncouth rhyme and shapeless
sculpture could do to preserve the memory of the
departed had been omitted. The scriptures had been
ransacked for consoling texts, and prose and verse
not only lavishly set down the virtues, talents, and

deeds of those described as "not lost but gone before," but also assiduously struggled to describe the emotions of the bereaved. Only once in all those generations had a strange reticence descended on the Clewer family. In the corner of the churchyard nearest to the house, directly beneath a darkly presiding yew tree, was a worn, flat stone. Here nothing implored the passing tribute of a sigh. There was only the bare inscription:

Here lyes the bodye of Elspeth Clewer.
Born 1550—dyed 1572.

And beneath, in different lettering, the words:

God grante that she lye stille.

This inscription struck me as laconic and queerly worded, so like, and yet so different, from the familiar *"Requiescat in pace."* Could those who buried the dead girl find nothing to praise? Was it too great a strain on their capacity for hope to associate her with peace? Or was the rather piteous supplication, "God grante that she lye stille," more for themselves than for her they consigned to the grave?

Idly I wondered whether I should ever know Margaret Clewer well enough to question her about this undesignated ancestress. It was now time to turn from the dead to the living, so I moved toward the home of the Clewers. As I approached the iron-studded door, the air was heavily sweet with the scent of the magnolias. These, as well as wisteria and clematis, clustered thickly over the front of the

Here Lyef The Body
OF
ELSPETH CLEW
BORN 1550   dyed 15
God grant that she lye ftille

building, but to my fancy the great house seemed to wear them with, as it were, a shrug of indifference, as though it knew nothing could really enhance its own beauty. The gentle austerity of that beauty humbled me again, and it was with a sense of intrusion that I pulled the bell and heard the responding clang and the bark of an aroused dog.

I don't know what I had subconsciously expected, but the smiling, beribboned parlormaid who opened the door seemed incongruous.

"Doctor Stone?" she asked. "Miss Clewer is expecting you."

Obedient to her "Come this way, please," I followed through a large hall in which young people were playing Ping-Pong and noisy games of cards, the blare of a Gramophone triumphing over the confusion of sounds. A heavy door through which we passed cut us off into complete cool silence, and a short flight of shiny black oak stairs, splendidly solid to the tread, led us to the door of my patient's room. The strong evening sun streamed in and it was through a dance of dazzling motes that I first saw her.

She lay on a low, wide bed drawn close up to the window, and a golden retriever luxuriously sprawled over the flower-embroidered coverlet that was spread across her feet.

I cannot remember how much I took in at first sight; I know the window shelf and the tables were then, as always, crowded with flowers and great branches cut from trees, and the bed strewn with books, writing materials, and needlework.

The shock with which I saw her was not without an element of recognition. Vaguely I had always expected that one day I should see a woman far more lovely than all others. Her hair gleamed in the sunshine, and her translucent face smiled up at me. I thought I should never see anything more beautiful, but I did the next time I saw her, for the variety of her beauty was unending. Changing as the sea changes with the sky, her coloring had its special response to every tone of light, just as her expression varied with every shade of feeling. It was a fluid, unset loveliness, suggesting far more than it asserted.

After this first sight of her I was often to wonder how I should describe her, supposing I had to reduce my impressions to the scope of words. What, for instance, should I set down if I were asked to fill in her passport? Would she be allowed across frontiers if I described her mouth as normal? Normal!—when it was never the same for two consecutive seconds. As for her eyes—I should not even have known what color to call them.

> Eyes too mysterious to be blue,
> Too lovely to be gray

would not help. Many more than two colors met in those pools of light.

As I entered the room I was to know so well, two canaries in a large golden cage were singing loudly, and I could scarcely hear Margaret Clewer's welcoming words. In her lovely, lilting, but to my professional ear, definitely nervous voice, before she began to speak of herself, she asked me many questions as to the comfort of my house and my impressions of my new practice. I had almost forgotten in what capacity I was there when she said, "I've been very silly and strained my heart, I think, over-rowing myself. I've got a craze for very violent exercise. Anyhow, I feel distinctly queer, and my heart seems to beat everywhere where it shouldn't be. And so," she added in her way—how well I was to know that way —of speaking in inverted commas, "my friends insist on my taking medical advice, so perhaps you had better see if my heart is in the right place."

It did not take me long to discover that her heart was severely strained. There was also a very considerable degree of anemia, and I prescribed three weeks' rest in bed.

My verdict was received with equanimity.

"If I can't row or ride, I'd just as soon remain in the horizontal," she answered gaily. "I shall be quite happy with books and food and friends, and with my beautiful Sheen. Isn't he lovely?" she added, turning the retriever's golden head toward me.

After paying homage, I asked if there were anyone to whom she would like me to speak about her health.

"Oh, no! I haven't any relations. I haven't anyone to edit me. I'm quite alone."

"But there seem so many people in the house."

"Oh, yes, but they're just visitors. When I said

'alone,' I meant 'independent.' I couldn't bear to be literally alone."

The last words were said with a vehemence that rather surprised me. Her room, with its multitude of books, a violin, and several unfinished sketches, seemed to bear evidence of such varied resources, and I had already diagnosed her as a person who would be very good company to herself.

As I shook hands with her, saying I would return the day after tomorrow, I noticed that for all their brightness, the responsive eyes held a slightly—not exactly hurt, but shall I say "initiated" expression? In spite of the nervous voice, my first impression had been that here, if anywhere, was one who had not felt the touch of earthly years. This superficial impression was already modified. Had life already bared its teeth at this lovely girl?

"I saw you groping about among the graves," she said as I reluctantly turned toward the door. "Are you interested in the rude forefathers, in worms and graves and epitaphs?"

"Well, at any rate, I love epitaphs," I replied, "and this is a peculiarly picturesque churchyard. You, yourself, must surely have a weakness for it, as you occupy a room so immediately overlooking it."

"Yes, I am close, aren't I?" She laughed. "No rude forefather could turn in his grave without my hearing him. But this happens to be the room I like best in the house. There isn't any harm in being so close, is there?"

"I can't say I consider it physically unhealthy," I

answered her professionally.

She smiled her swift, slanting smile. "Are you afraid of my being troubled by ghosts, Doctor Stone? Well, if it's a nervous patient you want, I'll see what I can do to oblige you; but first, please put my heart back into the right place."

I told her I would do my best and return the day after tomorrow to report progress.

"*Au revoir*, then," she said. "And meanwhile I shall look out for you in the churchyard, you ghoul! You ought to come and see it by night. You can't think how lovely it is in the moonlight, with a great white owl swooping and brushing against the tombstones."

As I turned my back on the beautiful house I found myself walking with a light step. For the first time since I came to this friendless new country a fellow creature had made me aware of myself as a human being. Till then I had been merely the new doctor.

I walked back through the village with a sense of enhanced life. There was now something to which I looked forward.

I visited my new patient three times during the next week. Finding her physical condition very little improved, I decided that some electric treatment would be beneficial, and as I had a portable apparatus, I was able to give the applications in her own room. A long course of this treatment involved many visits, which were the occasion for the most enchanting talks I have ever known. I look back on these summer weeks as the happiest of my life. Day after day I drifted on a stream of delight. She was a

magical companion, to me a real Pentecost. Her
quicksilver sympathy, the lightning gaiety of her
response, her dancing voice, and a way she had of
appreciatively echoing one's last words—I suppose
it was all these qualities that made me for the first
time in my life feel so delightfully articulate. There
can never have been a more receptive and therefore
stimulating mind. It was as though she understood
my thoughts almost before I had decided to put
them into words.

There seemed no limitations to her understanding
and sympathy. Her supple mind rejected nothing,
and her iridescent gaiety was like running water in
sunshine, continually flinging off a lovely spray of
laughter. How, I wondered, had she found time to
read so widely, so richly to store her astonishing
verbal memory? Of herself she spoke very little in
any autobiographical way. After weeks of frequent
conversation I knew nothing of the events of her
life, of her dead parents, or of her friends. But almost
from the very beginning she showed a tendency to
discuss herself psychologically, to expatiate on her
character, or, rather, on what—to my amusement—
she called her *lack* of character.

I suppose it was about six weeks after my first visit
that our conversation took a turn which for me
sounded the first faint note of disquiet.

In her usual rather unconcerned voice she said,
"It must be fun to be someone very definite and positive. You can't think how uncomfortable it is to have
no personality."

I laughed. "Are you suggesting that you have none? I know of no one of whose personality one is more quickly and lastingly aware."

"I'm not fishing," she said with the slightest tinge of impatience. "I don't mean that I'm too insignificant and colorless to make any impression on other people. I know I'm quite nice to look at. I'm not stupid, and I've plenty of responsiveness. I don't know how to explain, but what I mean is that there is no real permanent essential me. Of course, I've got plenty of facets, and your presence conjures up a certain me—not too bad a one. Thank you for the self with which you temporarily endow me. But I don't feel any sense of being a separate entity. No—I can't find any essential core of personality, nothing which is equally there when I'm alone, with you, or with other people. . . . There's no real continuity. I'm so hopelessly fluid!"

"But—if I may say so," I broke in, "it is that very fluidity of your mind that makes it such a treat to talk to you. We were discussing Keats's letters the other day. Do you remember where he writes: 'The only means of strengthening one's intellect is to make up one's mind about nothing—to let the mind be a thoroughfare for all thoughts—not a select party'? I think—"

"No, no. I don't mean that sort of thing at all. You entirely misunderstand me!" she interrupted, and something in her face made me realize the subject was serious to her and that the characteristic lightness of her manner hid real concern.

"I'm not worrying about my qualifications as a companion," she continued. "You see, the difficulty is that I can't talk about myself in a serious voice. I always sound so flippant. But my flippancy is a reflex. I should like to be able to talk to you about myself really melodramatically."

"Please do," I urged. "I'm feeling quite serious."

"I don't expect I'll be able to, but let me try," she said. "I don't want to be a bore, but I assure you it really is nightmarish—this sense of having no identity. You remember the very first time I saw you, I told you that I couldn't bear to be alone?"

"Yes."

"Well, that is because other people seem to a certain extent to hold me together—to, as it were, frame me by, I suppose, their conceptions of me. But often when I'm quite by myself I feel like—like water released from a broken bowl—something just spilling away, to be reabsorbed back into nothingness. It's almost like a temporary dissolution—a lapsing away. Yes, lapsing is the word—lapsing back into nothingness."

"I don't think there is anything so very unusual about your sensations," I said, I fear rather pompously. "I think we all at times feel something very like what you describe. It's a mild sort of neurosis, and it's in the nature of every neurosis to give the sufferer a sense of singularity."

"I daresay," she said and went on as though making up her mind to take a fence. "But then, you see, I have twice had a strangely disturbing experience which has made those sensations I try to describe become a real obsession."

"Experiences?" I echoed. "What do you mean?"

"I'll tell you," she said. "Don't expect a ghost story. I should hate to raise false hopes. It will be difficult to describe these experiences, and I don't expect you'll believe me, but they are true. Anyhow, don't interrupt. Just let me Ancient-Mariner you. The first time was when I was very young—scarcely grown up. Late one evening I was resting on my bed. I was very tired and consequently especially depressed by that curiously disagreeable feeling I have tried to describe—the 'no identity' feeling. Like any other trouble, it is apt to be worse when I am over-tired.

"It was dark and my window, against which the jasmine tapped, was on the ground floor. I slept downstairs then. Suddenly I had that sense we all know of being impelled to look in a certain direction. I turned and saw a dim face pressed against the window—peering through at me. I wasn't exactly frightened—just rather detachedly aware that my heart was thumping. Just then the moon slipped free from a fleece of clouds, so that I could see the face quite clearly. It was my own face!"

"What?" I broke in.

"Yes, Dr. Stone. Of that there was no doubt. One knows one's own face. My face was gazing at me —very intently, very wistfully—and as I stared, whatever it was that was outside shook its head very sadly. I hoped I was dreaming. I shut my eyes, but I couldn't keep them shut, and when I looked up

again it was still there, and now it wrung its hands,
oh, so mournfully.

"As I have said, it was my own face I saw through
the window, but did I—could I—myself look so miserable? I wanted to see myself, my own self—so I got
out of bed. I found my knees were trembling and I
swayed as I went up to my looking glass.

"I don't know how to make you believe what I
am going to tell you. Don't laugh. It was the most
awful shock. I found I could not see myself in the
glass. I stared and stared. I shook the glass. But my
reflection was not there. The pictures on the wall, the
corner of the cupboard, the birdcage, all the familiar
objects were reflected as usual, but I myself was not
there.

"It was still outside, and now it looked as though
it were trying to get in—to get back, but could not.
Terror came over me, and a feeling of faintness
against which I desperately struggled. Dizzily I left
my room, dragged myself upstairs, and went up to the
Chippendale mirror in the drawing room. The wide,
shining sheet of glass was hopelessly empty of what
I sought. What had happened to me that I had no
reflection? Surely the thing must be a delusion. Was
I insane? I can't describe the state of mind in which
I returned to my own room. I scarcely dared open
the door. To my infinite relief the face was no longer
looking through the window. I strode to the looking
glass. My reflection was there. Except that I looked
strangely wan, my face was as usual." She paused.
"That was the first time it happened. Shall I tell you

about the second time, or do you wish to certify me at once?"

"Go on," I said.

"It was about three years later. I was laid up in bed with a sprained ankle. I had been in a sort of apathy all day and toward evening was assailed by that painful sense of the lack of identity that I have tried to describe. There seemed no string threading the beads of mere moods. I felt without any real opinion, emotion, or impulse, as though I were an actor thrust onto a stage without having been given a single word of his part. Just a sense of complete vacuum. Neither my mind nor my hands were engaged. I was not even consciously looking in any particular direction. Suddenly I found myself rigid and staring. There was a sofa in my room, and on it a form was lying just as I lay on my bed. The form was mine, and again my own face gazed at me —oh, so mournfully. As before, that awful sense of faintness—of ebbing away—came over me, but I just managed to remain conscious. It still lay on the sofa. The face gazed at me with an unforgettable look of sadness. It looked as though it wanted to speak—in fact, the lips moved—but I heard nothing. A hand mirror lay on a table within my reach, and I forced myself to lift it in front of my face. My dread was realized. I stared into blankness. My face was not reflected. For some time I lay there, now staring hypnotized at what lay on the sofa, now searching the empty mirror. I don't know how long it was before my reflection began mistily and gradually to reappear, flickering in and out until at last it was still and as usual—except that I looked as tired as I felt. Of course I didn't say anything about this to anyone. You are the first person I have mentioned it to. What is your verdict, Dr. Stone?"

"I am going to say a very tiresome thing," I replied, with a sense of the futility of my words as I pronounced them. "I think you dreamed both these experiences."

"If you are going to talk like that," she said wearily, "I shall never tell you anything about myself again. You know just as well as I do that I was awake."

"Well," I said, "you may not have been actually physically asleep, but I think this com—"

"If you are going to use the word *complex* I shall change my doctor!" she interrupted laughingly.

"I think," I continued, "that you had allowed this —what shall we call it?—obsession of yours about your lack of continuous personality to weigh so heavily on your subconscious mind that it created a sort of symbolic imagery which imposed itself on your senses even to the point of definite illusion. It was, so to speak, a fixation of an idea. This sort of phenomenon is quite well known to psychologists. I could give you many examples."

Margaret shook her head sadly. "It's sweet of you to try to reassure me, but I'm afraid I am not convinced. And," she added with darkening eyes, "this thing really troubles me far more than I have been able to convey. I think I told you I felt faint both times? Somehow I knew it was dreadfully important that I should not actually faint. With a desperate effort I held on to consciousness. I simply didn't dare let myself go and quite slip my moorings. It would be awful to be *ousted*, wouldn't it?"

"Ousted?" I echoed blankly.

"Well, isn't it rather a risk to leave untenanted bodies lying about? Houses need caretakers." She laughed, but there was no laughter in her eyes.

Before I left her she had dismissed the subject and become her familiar radiant self, and yet never again was I to feel quite untroubled about her. As for her "experiences," I dismissed them as purely subjective. Anything they might intimate was still for me too far removed in the regions of sheer fantasy. It was something in her voice when she used the word "ousted" that had made me conscious of a chill. That and the expression in her eyes. As usual I turned back to look at the house as I went out of the gate. The glow of the fading day warmed its gray austerity, and this evening, to my fancy, it wore an expression positively benign and sheltering.

I did not see much less of my patient after she ceased to be an invalid. Not only did I still give her electric treatment, but she would often ask me to dinner, and the happiest hours of my life were spent in her little sitting room, the most personal room I have ever known. It was like her very shell. I look back on those magic evenings of that late summer and see them in a golden haze. The white room heavy with the scent of flowers; the golden retriever, his plumed tail sweeping from side to side; Margaret in her shimmering beauty; the two of us talking—talking; or Margaret reading aloud, or at her piano playing by heart, gliding from one loveliness into another, characteristically never saying what it was that she was going to play. She frequently reverted to what she had told me on that day of sudden confidence, but usually very lightly, as though the matter no longer preyed on her mind. Once she even laughingly referred to herself as the "absentee landlady." Indeed, from the lulled expression of her eyes I judged her nerves to be much quieter, and it was a shock to me to realize how easily I had been deceived by the characteristic lightness of her manner. One evening she broke off in the middle of a poem she was reading aloud and said, "I am feeling very detached from myself this evening—disquietingly detached." She then began to harp on the old theme, dwelling on the affair of her reflection—the "homemade symbol," as we had agreed to call it. Her voice was unconcerned, and in an attempt at reassurance I said something rather perfunctory. At this she suddenly burst out with wholly unaccustomed vehemence, "From every word you say I know that you do not understand and that I can never make you understand!"

My chagrin at having failed her must have shown in my face.

"So sorry," she said in her sweetest manner. "How can you be expected to guess that I am serious when I can't help speaking even of these things in my

small-talk voice. I am such an involuntary bluffer!
But, you see, it happened again last night. But now,
for heaven's sake—" she broke in on my words of
concern, "for heaven's sake, don't let's say another
word about Margaret Clewer! Please read to me. I
want to get on with my embroidery."

I look back on that evening as the end of a halcyon
spell. The next morning stands out sharply etched
on my memory. From then onward it was through a
web of mystification, gradually thickening into horror
which baffled belief, that I struggled to preserve my
reason.

I had just finished my breakfast when I was told
Miss Clewer's maid wished to speak to me on the
telephone. I knew Rebecca Park well. She worshipped
her mistress, whom she had attended since childhood, and I was sure that, with the instinct of the
simple and devoted, she recognized me as a real
friend. Her voice was sharp with anxiety.

"Please come quick, sir. I can't wake my mistress
this morning, and her sleep don't seem natural."

Ten minutes later I entered the familiar bedroom.
Margaret lay in something between a swoon and a
sleep. She breathed unevenly, and I noticed that her
hands were tightly clenched.

No man who loves a woman can see her asleep
for the first time without emotion. Something
clutched at my heart as I looked at Margaret's un-
conscious face. I cannot remember whether I had
ever actually pictured her asleep. If so, I could never
have surmised that which I saw. How could closed

eyes and lack of color effect so great though subtle a change in a familiar face? What was it in the expression of those lovely features that was so utterly alien—so disquietingly alien—to the Margaret I loved?

Struck by the coldness of her wrist when I felt her pulse, I told Rebecca to fetch a hot-water bottle, and as we turned back the bedclothes to apply it we both received a shock. Margaret's feet were not only ice-cold, but damp and stained with earth. Little lumps of clay soil stuck between the toes. It had been a very wet night.

"She has been walking in her sleep," I whispered to Rebecca. "On no account tell her when she wakes, and please wash all traces from her feet. Quick, before she wakes."

I bathed her blue-veined temples. Margaret gave a long, shuddering sigh and very piteously breathed out, "No. No! *No!*" her voice rising as she pleaded.

As she recovered consciousness and the long lashes lifted, her own expression swam into her eyes like some lovely flower rising to the surface through muddied waters. Her first words were curious, and at the time I wondered whether Rebecca noticed.

"Is it me?" she said, gazing upward. Not, as I might have expected—for my presence must have puzzled her—"Is it you?" but "Is it *me?*"

I explained my presence, telling her as unconcernedly as possible that I had been sent for because she had fainted.

Her brow contracted and fear looked out of her eyes. As soon as Rebecca had left the room she spoke in the quick, level voice that I associated with her rare confidences.

"It happened again last night."

"What happened?"

"I was pushed out of myself—no reflection—nothing. You know I told you before how desperately hard whatever was left of me had to struggle not to faint. Well, this time I fainted. The awful dizziness overcame me. I had to let go." She gave a queer little laugh. "Yes, this time I really slipped my moorings and evidently my faint—as you call it—has lasted an unconscionable time. Not that I know when it was I went off. 'Went off' is the correct expression, isn't it?"

Impressing on Rebecca the necessity for absolute quiet, I started on my professional rounds, but not for one moment in all that busy day did the thought of Margaret leave my mind. An undefined but deep anxiety settled in my heart.

I have already admitted that I loved her. To hope for a return of my love had never entered my head. It did not occur to me that I could lay any claim to so transcendent a being. As soon would I have made a declaration to the moon. Fool that I was! How often I have asked myself whether avowed love might have helped where friendship failed.

At about half-past twelve that night I suddenly awoke, thoughts of Margaret thrumming in my brain. Suppose she were to walk in her sleep again? Might she not injure herself or wake up and be terrified? How could I have risked such a thing happening again without even warning her? Of course I should have arranged for someone to sleep in her room. I was in my clothes almost before I knew I had decided to go to the Manor House. If I found her walking I could lead her home in her sleep. A full moon flooded the house with a strange green beauty. Glancing up at Margaret's window, I was surprised to see it shut on so warm a night. I decided to patrol the courtyard and watch the door in case she should emerge. I trod as softly as possible. Save for the distant bark of the inevitable dog, my vigil seemed unshared. The night was full of an indescribable menace. A low wind crept through the trees and the leaves whispered momentously. Claimed by the moon, the house looked wan and remote, palely repudiating any human allegiance it might seem to concede by daylight. I was startled by the loud hoot of an owl, a sound I can never hear without a strange stirring as of some forgotten but intense memory. "You can't think how lovely it looks at night with a great white owl sweeping about." I remembered Margaret's words and obeyed an impulse to enter the churchyard. A white owl almost brushed my cheek as he passed on his blundering flight.

Beneath the transmuting moon the crowded tombstones looked more sharply outlined, far less merged into the green quiet of the long grass. In the daytime the atmosphere breathed a sense of acquiescence, as though the oft-repeated text, "Thy will be done," had been instilled into the very air. But now the peace of buried centuries seemed disturbed, the consecrated ground to quiver with insubmission. Even the yew trees seemed to bristle. Starkly black, they stood like mutinous sentinels.

As I turned my eyes to the eastern side of the churchyard, I heard myself gasp. In the uttermost corner something white glimmered on the ground. I knew at once what it was. Ten strides brought me to where Margaret, in her long nightgown, lay outstretched across a flat tombstone. Her arms, the hands tightly clenched, were flung out in front; her slim, protesting body writhed. It looked as though she were struggling to rise, but had no power—almost as though some force were drawing her down. I heard a low, piteous moaning and knelt to examine her pale, twisted face. The eyes were closed. Her tormented body rolled over to one side, leaving the inscription on the gray lichened stone exposed. As I knelt I involuntarily read the brief words:

> *Here lyes the bodye of Elspeth Clewer.*
> *God grante that she lye stille.*

I recalled my first visit to the churchyard. So it was upon the grave of Elspeth Clewer, the uncommended ancestress who had so aroused my curiosity, that Margaret lay.

"No! No! *No!*" was wrung from her lips, and she writhed as though in anguish.

I raised her gently. Strength was required. It was like lifting a body from quicksand. Fearful of waking her, I slowly led her home and to her room.

Sheen, the golden retriever, greeted me sleepily

but with his usual exquisite courtesy, and when I
had laid her on the bed, he gently licked his mistress's
white hand. I watched by her side for some time
until her sleep seemed tranquil and normal. Then,
in misplaced confidence, I left her alone, except for
the dog who lay stretched out his golden length
across the bed. Anxious to see her the next morning,
I went round as early as possible, intending to explain
my uninvited visit by a wish to alter a prescription.
But Rebecca met me in the passage, her honest brow
besieged with worry.

"You're a glad sight for sore eyes, Doctor. I was
just going to send for you. Miss Margaret's just like
she was yesterday—deep drowned in that sleep that
don't seem natural. I can't abide to see her like that."

"I think it only means she's very over-tired," I
said, anxious to soothe.

"That's as may be," she answered, unconvinced.
"Though what she's done to get so tired, I don't
know. And, Doctor, there's something most dreadful's gone and happened. I suppose that dratted cat
must have got into my lady's room in the night and
forced its way—the cunning brute—into the birdcage,
and there's them two sweet little birds, as Miss
Margaret sets such store by, lying dead in their
blood with their poor little heads torn right off of
their bodies. Really, I don't know how to tell Miss
Margaret when she wakes. She'll take on so!"

"I'll tell her," I said as I followed into the bedroom,
hastily adding, "but, for heaven's sake, take away the
cage. She mustn't see that sight when she wakes."

With little moans of concern the maid hurried away with her gruesome burden.

Margaret lay in deep unconsciousness. Her appearance was in every way the same as on the previous morning. I turned over her limp hand to feel her pulse. Then I heard my heart hammering in my ears. It was as though it had attended and taken in something my mind refused to accept. Soon I felt deadly sick. Self-protection, reason, fought against the evidence of my sight, but in vain. The lovely white hand that I had so often ached to kiss was thickly smeared with red, and sticking between the fingers and thumb was a cluster of bloodstained feathers.

For the first time I knew what it was to shudder with my whole being. Difficult though it was to control my thoughts, prompt action was necessary, and, fetching warm water, I hastily washed all traces from her hand.

Soon afterward she turned and, struggling through layers of oblivion and subconsciousness, came to herself. Bewilderment showed in her eyes, then relief and welcome.

"What's the matter?" she said, looking closely at my face.

Struggling to hide the shrinking that I felt, I explained my presence and wrote out a prescription.

Margaret looked round the room for her inseparable companion. "Where's Sheen?" she asked.

"He wasn't in here when I come in this morning, miss," said Rebecca, "and I can't find him nowhere.

I've asked everyone, and no one's seen him."

"He must have jumped out of the window," said Margaret. "How queer of him."

At her request I looked out of the window. The flower bed below plainly showed a dog's paw marks.

"I must get up and go and hunt for him," said Margaret. "I had a horrid dream about him."

She looked deathly pale, quite unfit to leave her bed, but I knew it would be useless to attempt to detain her. I had come to the conclusion that I must tell her of her sleepwalking and insist that she should have a night nurse for a time. I wanted an opportunity to break this to her as unalarmingly as possible, so I reminded her of her promise to call on a farmer's wife and try to persuade the obstinate woman to obey my injunctions and send her crippled child to a hospital. She agreed to come that afternoon.

As I left the house I remembered that I had not told her about the death of the birds—neither had she noticed the absence of their cage.

At three o'clock we started on our two-mile walk across the fields. It was a lovely afternoon, resplendent summer, though a delicious tang in the air hinted at autumn and brought an exquisite pink to Margaret's cheeks. More than ever I was struck by her astonishing look of dewy youth. Like a just-opened wild rose, her face looked utterly unused, as though it had never harbored any expression save one of vague expectancy. My horrid misgivings began to seem fantastically unreal.

"Have you heard of the cat's crime?" she asked.

Her eyes looked like wet flowers and her voice quivered, though characteristically she tried to laugh as she added, "Of all Shakespeare's adjectives, I think the queerest are his 'harmless' and 'necessary' applied to a cat. I adored those little birds."

I murmured sympathy.

"I'm wretchedly worried about Sheen's disappearance, too," she said. "He's never been away from me for even an hour before. He'll go mad with misery without me. Do you think he can have been stolen?"

"I'm quite sure he hasn't," I said emphatically.

I steered the conversation until, as unconcernedly as possible, I told her I had discovered that she was given to the quite common but not to be encouraged habit of sleepwalking.

Consternation flared in her eyes and she flushed painfully. She tried to laugh it off.

"I wonder what my particular 'damned spot' may be. It always is some damned spot that won't 'out' that makes people walk in their sleep—isn't it? Or may it be merely due to unsubmissive food?"

"It's far more often caused by indigestion than by conscience," I said with a laugh. I took advantage of this wave of flippancy to float the hospital nurse into the conversation.

To my surprise and relief Margaret promptly acquiesced. In fact, it seemed to me that a look of unmistakable relief flickered across her face. I told her an excellent nurse was just about to leave one of my patients, and that I would engage her to come in that evening.

"You won't need to see her at all during the day," I said. "She'll just sit up in your room at night."

"Oh, I hope she doesn't knit," laughed Margaret. "I don't expect sleep will ever slide into my soul with her sitting there. I shall be the watched pot that never boils! However, no sleep—no walking; so it will be all to the good."

With that we dismissed the matter.

"Now let's forget everything except this winged hour. It is such a heavenly afternoon!" she exclaimed. "Thank heaven I can always live in the present. I hope you don't think it's dreadful to have a nature like a duck's back."

She stepped out and the shadow which had over-hung her ever since that unexpected outburst in her sitting room lifted from her. Once more she shone out as the radiant being I had first known. It was im-possible not to be infused by her brilliant gaiety, and as her lovely peals of laughter rang out, for the time being my nightmare was almost dispersed. Her inimitable mimicry, delicious raillery, and stream of brilliantly garbled quotations almost made me for-get the unforgettable. But her radiance suddenly clouded over when I said: "What an amazing memory you have!"

"Memory?" she answered almost sharply. "Yes, I admit I have plenty of memory and understand-ing. But what protection are such merely *receptive* qualities?"

"Protection?" I echoed blankly.

"Well, here we are," she said in evasion, her hand

on the farmyard gate. "Now I propose that you stay
here, while I go in by myself and twist the good
woman round my little finger. I'm sure your presence
would cramp my little finger's style. Please wish it
luck." And, pulling off her glove, she smilingly held
up her tapering, pink-nailed finger. "What's the matter?" she asked uneasily.

I'm afraid an uncontrollable inward shudder must
have shown on my face. The last time I had looked
at that slender finger it had been stained with blood,
and I could still see the pitiful little feathers that had
stuck to it.

"I've got a stitch," I lied. "I'll wait here for your
good news. Good luck."

A prey to uninvited thoughts, I leaned against the
gate.

About five minutes later I heard myself hailed
and was delighted to see the gardener with Sheen
on a chain. As I patted the beautiful dog's head, he
slowly waved his sweeping tail.

"Please, sir," explained the gardener, "the keeper
found him in a distant wood, and when he brings
him home, Miss Park, knowing where you was goin',
she asks me to follow you, thinking Miss Clewer
would be that pleased to see him safe."

Delighted to be the bearer of good news, I hurried
toward the farmhouse and was met by Margaret.

"Triumph to my little finger!" she began, but as
soon as I spoke of Sheen her successful mission was
forgotten in delight, and she ran toward the gate.
"Darling, darling Sheen! How could you leave

me?" I heard her eager voice.

Then something dreadful happened—something so painful that even now I can scarcely endure to recall it.

As Margaret approached her dog, expecting an exuberant welcome, an unaccountable change came over him. His tail was lowered until it disappeared between his cringing legs, and his whole body shook with unmistakable terror.

"Sheen—what *is* the matter?"

Her voice was piteous and, looking at her face, I saw it contorted with unbearable suffering.

"It's *me!*" she pleaded. "Sheen, it's *me!*"

But the dog she had said "would be mad with misery without her" cowered lower and lower as though it would creep through the ground.

"Oh, what did happen last night?" wailed Margaret, and she put out her hands to the dog in anguished propitiation.

"Back, miss, back!" shouted the terrified gardener.

The dog's eyes showed white, he howled, snapped wildly in Margaret's direction, and tore at his collar in frantic efforts to escape.

"Take him away!" cried Margaret. "Take him away! I'll go back by the road." And she started off as fast as her swift stride could carry her.

I overtook her, but could think of nothing to say. A terrible constraint lay between us. I looked at her. Tears coursed down her white, strained face, and her mortally affronted eyes stared straight in front.

"Unaccountable things, dogs," at last I ventured.

"Unaccountable? Do you think so?" she said sharply. "I wonder." And as she strode on, she clenched her hands till the knuckles stood out white.

A moment later she turned to me as though she were on the point of really speaking, of letting something gush out. She made a little movement with one hand, but then it was as though an iron shutter slid between us, and in a cold, formal voice she told me of her successful interview with the farmer's wife. That was all we spoke of. We might have been almost strangers.

The next morning I went to give her some electric treatment. She looked bitterly troubled, but said she liked the hospital nurse, a pleasant, serene-faced young woman. I missed the accustomed twitter of the birds, and the room looked strangely deserted without the beautiful golden dog. I dared not ask about him, and I never saw him again.

With a pang of pity I noticed that all the mirrors had been removed.

"Has that queer thing happened again?" I ventured. "Did you think there was something wrong with your reflection?"

"Don't ask me about that anymore," she answered feverishly. "I've finished with all that fanciful nonsense and I never wish to hear it alluded to again. Never, never, never!"

With that, a safety curtain of unhappy reserve fell between us. She seemed to consign herself to the loneliness of utter withdrawal, and from that time onward the shadows settled more and more darkly on her beautiful face.

A few days after her arrival I asked the nurse to come and talk to me about her patient. She had nothing very definite to report, except that, though her charge slept for a fair number of hours, her sleep was very troubled and brought little refreshment. In fact, she always seemed most tired and overwrought in the mornings.

"Of course," she said, "I do think that having no fresh air in the room these stifling hot nights may have something to do with her condition."

"Why," I asked, "do you mean to say she doesn't have the window open in this weather?"

The stubborn summer had blazed out in a last fierce spell of heat, and I was indeed amazed.

"No, sir, I can't persuade her to, and sometimes I can scarcely bear the closeness myself."

I promised to use my influence.

"Then there's another thing," the nurse went on. "Do you think it can be good for anyone in an excited state of nerves to be doing all that rehearsing? If you'll excuse my saying so, sir, I think you should order her to give up those theatricals."

"Theatricals?" I echoed. "What theatricals?"

"I don't know when they're to be, but I know she's very busy rehearsing for them. Whenever she sends me to fetch something during the night—and she's always asking me to fetch some book or something special from the stillroom; not that she ever seems to use the things when I bring them—well, as I come back, all the way down that long passage, I hear her fairly screaming out her part. Wonderful actress she must be! You wouldn't really think it could be her own voice. No, you wouldn't think such a sweet young lady could produce so horrid a voice. It simply raises my hair—that acting voice of hers does. And, as I was saying, I really can't think it can be good for anyone whose nerves are disturbed to be studying so violent a part."

"Thank you, nurse. I'll speak about it."

That afternoon I called on Margaret. After some casual talk I said, "I hear you sleep with your window shut. And you know you are looking extremely pale. To insist on keeping the window open all the year round may be a foolish fetish, but in this sort of weather it really is essential."

"If the nurse makes a fuss about that I won't keep her," Margaret burst out. "How can I leave the window open when it's from there that I feel that awful pressing in—that pressing and pushing away? How can I? Though heaven knows it's foolish enough to think it's any use to shut things. 'If stone walls cannot a prison make, nor iron bars a cage,' still less can they make a fortress." Suddenly she seemed to remember herself. "But these are but 'wild and whirring words,'" she said, smiling. "I'm so sorry. Please don't pay any attention to them. My disease of quoting grows worse and worse. It's because I have no opinions of my own."

She looked disquietingly excited, and my own head swam. "That awful pressing in"? What did she, what could she, mean? A sense of dreadful menace almost stifled me, and I felt utterly estranged. But something had to be said.

"When are your theatricals to be?" I asked. "I didn't know you were acting."

"Acting?" she repeated. "What do you mean?"

"The nurse tells me she often hears you rehearsing in the night."

She blushed crimson. "Oh, that!" she said. "Oh, yes! You see, I have a silly habit of reciting poetry aloud to myself, and it made me feel self-conscious to know she had overheard me, so I said I was rehearsing for some theatricals."

"I see," I said. But my heart sank at hearing her lie.

Then we spoke of other things, but we were both hopelessly preoccupied, and there was no life in our talk. It was almost forced, and I noticed that nearly everything that Margaret said was in inverted commas. Scarcely anything passed her lips that was not a quotation. I had already observed that the more tired, strained, or preoccupied she seemed, the more this was the case. When her vitality was lowered it was, to use her own words, as though she had "no opinion, emotion, or impulse" of her own, but was merely a thoroughfare for the thoughts of others—as though nothing remained to hold the fort except memory.

I think it was three days later that the nurse, of her own accord, came to report to me again and told me she considered her patient increasingly nervous

and depressed. To my inquiry as to how Miss Clewer
was sleeping, she answered, "Very little now," adding
ominously, "and if you ask me, sir, I don't think she
wants to go to sleep."

"She's given up the theatricals, anyhow, hasn't
she?" I asked as casually as I could.

"Given them up, sir? No, I wish to goodness' sake
she would. I really can scarcely bear to hear it; the
way she screams out her part has thoroughly got on
my nerves. As often as I come back along that passage, she's going through it. I know some of her part
by heart myself. I don't believe I'll ever be able to
forget the queer words."

"What are the words you overhear her saying?"
I asked as indifferently as I could.

"Saying? You wouldn't call it 'saying' if you'd heard
her, sir. It's more like yelling. As I was saying the
other day, you'd never think such a gentle lady could
produce such a terrifying voice. The words that she
most often repeats are 'Let me in! Give way! What
can I do without a body? What use are you making
of your body? I want it! You clear out! I must be
lodged! I must be lodged! *I must be lodged!*' And the
third time she repeats 'I must be lodged,' her voice
rises to a screech. But whatever's the matter, sir?
You've come over as white as a sheet!"

Murmuring that I felt faint and must get some
brandy, I told her I would see her in the evening and
left the room.

My legs almost gave way as I went upstairs, and
as soon as I reached my bedroom I turned the key

in the lock, though what it was I thought might thus be debarred, God only knows! With shaking hands I opened the book I had been reading in bed the night before.

It was a bound copybook, filled with the faded brown of a spidery sixteenth-century writing. Margaret had long given me the freedom of her library, and on a high shelf I had found a manuscript book —a sort of irregular journal kept by an ancestress of hers, also a Margaret Clewer. I had read it far into the night. It was all interesting, and by the final heartbroken entry I had been most vividly and painfully impressed. Were certain words really as, with horror, I remembered them, or was my memory deceiving my disturbed nerves?

Trembling, I turned the leaves until I came to the words:

So she is dead! Elspeth, our shame, lyes dead. That I should live to thank God that my own child be laid in the churchyarde! A sennight yesterday since they carryed her home after her falle from her horse. A sennight of torment unimagined to us all. The passing of her eville spirit has been a horror past beliefe. The drawing nigh of Death had no softening effect on her violent, eville, greedy spirit. Her hold on lyfe was terrible. Breath by breath it was torne from her shattered bodye. So her fierce spirit clung to her beautiful broken bodye. God helpe us all! Could any Death be deep enough to make me to forget how with her last breaths she cryde out: "I won't dye! I won't dye! There is still so much to do! Some way I'll get back! I must get back! My spirit is so unquenched! I *must* find another bodye. I must be lodged! I must be lodged! *I must be lodged!*"

The long-dead woman's manuscript slipped from

my hand, and I struggled to think. Even last night the words of the dying changeling daughter had made me shiver. Now, after what the nurse had quoted, they seared my mind. Elspeth Clewer! I remembered the gray, uncommunicative grave beneath the yew tree. Its bleak reticence had impressed my imagination on my first visit to the churchyard, and now, to my mind's eye, it was forever associated with Margaret's prostrate, writhing body.

"God grante that she lye stille! God grante that she lye stille!" I snatched at a faint, fluttering hope. Perhaps Margaret was familiar with the journal I had found. If so, its grim contents would be very likely to haunt her. Might not what the nurse mistook for rehearsing have been her quoting it in disturbed sleep?

That evening I found her pale and wild-eyed. I told her of my discovery of the diary and asked if she had ever read it. She disclaimed all knowledge, and this time I knew she spoke the truth. I said it gave a strange account of an ancestress of hers—an Elspeth Clewer. Was it my fancy, or did she draw in her breath at the name?

"Oh, does it?" she said. "Yes, I've heard of her. Though she died before she was twenty-three, she's the only celebrated member of the Clewer family, for she crowded her short life with every imaginable vice and crime. I believe she was an absolute mythical monster of violence and cruelty, but as I have often told you, I really don't take the faintest interest in my ancestors."

Two days later, as I sat at breakfast, the front doorbell was so violently pulled that I went to the door myself. The faithful Rebecca stood there, her face mottled with agitation.

"Oh, sir! She's been and gone and bolted!"

"Miss Clewer?" I gasped.

"No, sir," she gabbled breathlessly. "That yere nurse, been and gone and offed it—left my poor lamb with no word to no one. Yes, when I comes along this mornin' I finds my lady deep asleep, and, if you please, on the floor there's a tray with broken pieces of cup and saucer and Benger's food slopped all over the carpet. Just dropped out of the nurse's hand, it must have been. And she couldn't be found nowhere; clean gone, she was—run off and left all her things behind her. The garden boy, he tells me he seen her tearing round the garden like as though the devil were after her. I looks in at the station, and they said she'd been there a full hour before the first train went and looked that queer without no hat nor nothing. And my lady—she looks to go to your heart this morning—she says she calls to mind asking the nurse to fetch her a cup of Benger's, and then she thinks she must have fallen asleep, since she doesn't remember no more."

Incensed with the nurse, I rang up the London association from which she came and instructed them to telephone as soon as she arrived. Full of foreboding, I hurried to the Manor House. I found Margaret walking up and down in the garden, her face drawn and set.

"I'm sorry I've frightened your nurse away," she said bitterly.

"Frightened her? You?" I tried to laugh.

"So it seems. A well-trained nurse who drops her tray and flies from the house must be a little upset."

"She must have taken leave of her senses," I said dryly. "Fortunately I know of an admirable one who happens to be free now."

"No, thank you. No more nurses for me! I can't say I've found the last one very reassuring. No, I've just telegraphed to lots of my friends to come down. I've been too unsociable lately." She spoke defiantly, and I knew it would be no use to argue.

That afternoon I was rung up by the matron of the nursing association. Nurse Newson had never turned up, but on inquiry it was found she had gone to her mother, whose telephone number I was given.

"Mrs. Newson speaking," answered a painstakingly genteel voice.

I explained who I was, stating that I wished to speak to her daughter, whose amazing behavior demanded explanation.

The voice let itself go, and unmistakable relish of a crisis was plain through its agitation.

"Oh, sir! I'm afraid you can't speak to my daughter. She's bad in bed, and Doctor says she's suffering from shock and mustn't be disturbed. Oh, sir, whatever did happen to make her take on so, such a sensible, steady girl as she is? She's in ever such a state! I never did see anyone so upset before, and I can't get from her what it is she's so scared of—

at least nothing that you would call coherent. And, please, sir, she says she's terribly sorry to have let you down, but she couldn't have stayed on—not for any consideration."

Feeling no sympathy, I snapped out, "I never heard of such behavior. A nurse abandoning a case in the middle of the night. She must be hopelessly hysterical. What possible excuse can she have? Her patient is the most charming young lady."

"Yes, she says the young lady she was engaged for was ever so sweet, but, Doctor—I don't understand—she talks so wild—and when I question her, begs me not to ask, but wasn't there *another* young lady?"

Exasperated, I banged the receiver down.

It was necessary to go to the Manor House to give the address to which the nurse's luggage was to be sent. I would have gone in, but two cars were just unloading their freight of visitors. Loud voices echoed in the courtyard, and aggressive young people, brandishing tennis rackets, bounded up the steps toward their hostess, who stood in the doorway, her face resolutely gay.

With a forlorn sense of being cut off from her and with apprehension heavy on my heart, I stole away. As I looked back at the house, gilded by the setting sun, I almost hated it for its unconcerned beauty.

Two days later I received a note in her strangely variable but always recognizable writing. It had no beginning.

I am going away. I must leave at once. When you get this I shall be in the train. I could not stay here another night. Please never ask me to explain. Something unthinkably dreadful happened last night. I could never dare risk having anyone stay here again. Not possibly.

Neither can I live here by myself.

I don't understand, but, believe me, it's fearful, and I must go. Oh, God! There *are* more things in heaven and earth!

I'll write.

Margaret Clewer

She went abroad, and I was glad to know her gone. If life became unutterably dreary, at least my nightmare fears were in abeyance. Naturally I wrote begging for an explanation of her note, but none came. I had many letters from her, but, except for the one line, "I am so glad I came away," they told me nothing. They were merely brilliant descriptions of her travels—little more than inspired Baedekers, with scarcely a word to show we had ever been great friends and shared an unacknowledged dread. I wrote to Rebecca to inquire after her mistress's health. Her reply said her young lady seemed well enough, but appeared restless and as though not really enjoying the full life she led.

As the leaves fluttered down, till winter lay like iron over the land, the magical days of that long summer began to assume the golden haze of something dreamed. Often I would go and gaze at her empty home. I began to wonder whether I was ever to see her again. There was even a rumor that the Manor House was to be let on a long lease.

One morning, when an unusually reluctant spring had at last turned the fields to glory, I was surprised to see on an envelope bearing a London postmark the writing that always made my heart leap. I read:

> I find it quite impossible to keep away any longer. I feel myself irresistibly drawn home, but I shall not sleep in my old room. I shall come back Monday, but shall arrive late. Please come to luncheon Tuesday.
>
> Margaret Clewer

Coming home Monday? This was Monday. I should see her in little more than twenty-four hours. The day crept by with unbelievable slowness. To hasten to-morrow I went to bed unusually early.

In the middle of the night I woke up suddenly and with the certainty that I had been aroused by some sound. Yes, there it was again, outside the house. Small pebbles were being thrown up against my window. Expecting an emergency call, I struggled out of sleepiness and looked out of my low window. The moon was full; a tall figure stood below; a white, upturned face gleamed in the silvery green light. It was Margaret! Her loveliness glimmered in the strange, cold night, but she looked wild, and there was desperate urgency in her voice.

"Quick, quick!" she cried. "I must have your help. I'm so frightened. Quick! Let me in! Let me in! This time I'll tell you everything!"

Snatching my overcoat, I hurried downstairs as

quietly as I could, for fear of waking my servant, and opened the door.

It was no dream. The white figure stood outside, the arms outstretched toward me. A glorious hope leapt in my heart, but as I advanced something indescribable looked out of her eyes. With desperate haste her hands moved, and in a second her face was entirely concealed by the chiffon scarf in which they had swathed it.

"Too late! Too late!" she wailed in a changing voice. "Go back, go back, and for God's sake don't dare to follow me!" The white figure sped away.

Aghast, I started in pursuit, but after a few strides the swathed, faceless figure turned. At the torrent of words that were shrieked at me in an unknown voice, I stood transfixed, frozen with horror. Wild, nauseated fear took possession of me. God forgive me, I renounced her. To save my soul I could not have followed another step. I stole back and, drenched in cold sweat, lay shaking on my bed. Sleep never approached me, but I felt too shattered and ill to get up at my usual hour. At ten the telephone rang. Wondering what ghastly intimation was to come, I lifted the receiver.

Margaret's lovely voice slid into my astonished ears.

"It's *me*. Please come and see me. They tell me I'm not well."

Her own lovely voice that I had not hoped to hear again. Had some monstrous dream imposed itself upon me? Almost I began to think it.

When I reached the Manor House, I asked where Miss Clewer's new room was.

"Just the same as before, sir," replied the parlormaid. "Miss Clewer did give orders for one to be prepared on the other side of the house, but as soon as she came she said she'd go back to her own room."

Rebecca lay in wait in the familiar passage.

"Thank God you've come, Doctor," she whispered. "Miss Margaret seems to be wandering in her mind this morning."

I stole into the room. Margaret, strangely beautiful but wan and fragile, lay back on a great pillow. She stretched out both hands in welcome. At once I knew that her memory held no trace of last night. She greeted me as though we met for the first time since her departure all those long months ago.

"Rebecca thinks I'm ill," she said. "But I must be a creature incapable of my own distress, because I assure you I feel quite well and, oh, so, so glad to see my physician!"

Did I say that, after the incident of the dog, I was only once again to see Margaret in her incomparable radiance? Strange that it should have been now, when I was prepared to find her in delirium. But thus it was. Once more she seemed her original, untroubled, sparkling self.

She questioned me about all the Mosstone news and gave irresistibly funny descriptions of people she had met on her travels. All was as I first remembered her: dancing voice; lovely laughter; buoyant, bubbling talk; lightning response; showers of quotations. What had Rebecca meant by describing her as delirious?

But suddenly a change came into her eyes. She clutched at my hands and held them tight. Then she began to do what Rebecca described as wandering. Her own voice was solemn.

"As the tree falls, so shall it lie! That is true, isn't it, John?" John? I had almost forgotten my unused Christian name. "It is true in every sort of way," she went on, "isn't it, darling? And as that tree lies, so shall it be all through the days of eternity—that's true, too, isn't it, John—absolutely true?"

"Yes—yes, of course," I soothed her.

"Oh, John," she went on, "I've just found such a lovely, lovely poem. I didn't know it before. I can't think how I could have missed it. It's by Barnefield. Just listen to the mournful magic of these two lines:

> "King Pandion he is dead,
> All thy friends are lapped in lead.

" 'Lapped in lead'! Doesn't that make death sound delicious and luxurious? As though to be alive were something very makeshift." She gave a little quick laugh. "Lapped in lead—lapped in lead," she repeated very slowly. "Oh, how lovely and peaceful and untormented! You know that would be the best thing that could happen to me, don't you? The best thing that could happen to your me. Then *your* me would be safe."

An urgent summons came, and I had to go to a distant case. Telling Rebecca on no account to leave her for a moment and that I would get a nurse to come as soon as possible, I hurried away.

It was for a birth that I had been summoned. The baby was as reluctant to enter the world as its mother seemed disposed to leave it, and midnight had already struck when I reached home.

Through all the strain of that endless day I had been haunted by Margaret, and I intended to snatch some supper and hurry back to the Manor House. But before I had sat down the telephone rang. It was Rebecca's voice.

"Come quick. Come at once! Miss Margaret seems so weak as though she couldn't scarcely breathe. I'm speaking from her room. Do—" The voice broke off; it was no longer at the mouthpiece, but I heard it cry out in deathly terror, "Oh, God, who—" And then the telephone must have been dropped.

No further sound came through. I replaced the receiver, and after a moment's pause rang up the exchange, in my impatience violently rattling the instrument. "Number, please; number, please," expostulated the exchange. I gave the number several times, but there was nothing to be heard beyond the intermittent cry of an unanswered call. . . . I pictured the overturned telephone lying on the floor of Margaret's room. What had happened?

Leaping into my car, I drove to the Manor House. The front door stood wide open, but no one was about. I did not meet anyone on my way to Margaret's room. The whole house was deserted.

What I saw when I approached the bed no one

could attempt to describe and keep his reason. It writhed and moaned and seemed to breathe with terrible difficulty. I averted my eyes from the face, and with the automatic professional instinct to preserve life, administered an injection.

The thing on the bed gave a convulsive shudder and I heard the fast, thick breathing of some desperate struggle. Determined not to see the usurper again, I kept my eyes shut. I dared not look! Then there was silence, followed by a gentle sigh.

Something in that gentle sigh impelled me to open my eyes. Ineffable relief flowed over me. Like pure silver rising through primeval slime, the being I loved had struggled through and triumphed over the awful spiritual hideousness of that invasion. It was Margaret's face that smiled at me. Her voice came sweet but hopelessly weak.

"It's all right, darling," she breathed, and in her voice was a tenderness I had never imagined. "It's all right. I've won. It's me, *your* me. Don't let me give way again. Keep me safe—"

Sure of her haven, she gazed at me. Her hand clung to mine and her lips smiled, but the strain of that final struggle had been too much for the already weakened heart. The eyelids fluttered up once or twice as her clasp of my hand loosened. Almost inaudibly, but with an ecstasy of glimpsed peace, she breathed out the words, "Lapped in lead, lapped in lead. . . ." And something else I could not quite hear. I felt a last little clinging clutch at my hand, and with one or two long sighs the spirit I loved slipped from its beautiful lodging.

Some hours later I left the deserted house and returned to the emptied world. Gratitude mingled with my grief; my broken heart was at peace, for I knew her to be unassailable. The long dread was at an end.

It is a desolate path I tread, but sometimes, when it seems most steep and bare, there comes, like a gentle wave washing against my tired brain, the soft assuagement of her voice murmuring, "Lapped in lead, lapped in lead." And again I hear the promise in the infinite tenderness of her whispered "Darling."

What were the words I failed to hear?

I often linger round her empty home. No smoke rises from the twisted chimneys, but pigeons still flutter and croon, and the gray house I once thought so aloof seems to receive me into an atmosphere of benign peace.

The Voice in the Night

William Hope Hodgson

IT WAS A DARK, starless night. We were becalmed in the northern Pacific. Our exact position I do not know, for the sun had been hidden during the course of a weary, breathless week by a thin haze which had seemed to float above us, about the height of our mastheads, sometimes descending and shrouding the surrounding sea.

With there being no wind we had steadied the tiller, and I was the only man on deck. The crew, consisting of two men and a boy, were sleeping forward in their den, while Will—my friend, and the master of our little craft—was aft in his bunk on the port side of the little cabin.

Suddenly, from out of the surrounding darkness, there came a hail: "Schooner, ahoy!"

The cry was so unexpected that I gave no immediate answer because of my surprise.

It came again—a voice curiously throaty and inhuman, calling from somewhere upon the dark sea away on our port broadside: "Schooner, ahoy!"

"Hello!" I sang out, having gathered my wits somewhat. "What are you? What do you want?"

119

"You need not be afraid," answered the queer voice, having probably noticed some trace of confusion in my tone. "I am only an old—man."

The pause sounded odd, but it was only afterward that it came back to me with any significance.

"Why don't you come alongside, then?" I queried somewhat snappishly, for I liked not his hinting at my having been a trifle shaken.

"I—I—can't. It wouldn't be safe. I—" The voice broke off, and there was silence.

"What do you mean?" I asked, growing more and more astonished. "Why not safe? Where are you?"

I listened for a moment, but there came no answer. And then, a sudden indefinite suspicion of I knew not what coming to me, I stepped swiftly to the binnacle and took out the lighted lamp. At the same time I knocked on the deck with my heel to waken Will. Then I was back at the side, throwing the yellow funnel of light out into the silent immensity beyond our rail. As I did so I heard a slight, muffled cry, and then the sound of a splash, as though someone had dipped oars abruptly. Yet I cannot say that I saw anything with certainty, save, it seemed to me, that with the first flash of the light there had been something upon the waters, where now there was nothing.

"Hello, there!" I called. "What foolery is this?"

But there came only the indistinct sounds of a boat being pulled away into the night.

Then I heard Will's voice, from the direction of the after scuttle: "What's up, George?"

"Come here, Will!" I said.

"What is it?" he asked, coming across the deck.

I told him the queer thing which had happened. He put several questions; then, after a moment's silence, he raised his hands to his lips and hailed: "Boat, ahoy!"

From a long distance away there came back to us a faint reply, and my companion repeated his call. Presently, after a short period of silence, there grew on our hearing the muffled sound of oars, at which Will hailed again.

This time there was a reply: "Put away the light."

"I'm damned if I will," I muttered. But Will told me to do as the voice bade, and I shoved it down under the bulwarks.

"Come nearer," he said, and the oar strokes continued. Then, when apparently some half-dozen fathoms distant, they again ceased.

"Come alongside," exclaimed Will. "There's nothing to be frightened of aboard here!"

"Promise that you will not show the light?"

"What's to do with you," I burst out, "that you're so infernally afraid of the light?"

"Because—" began the voice, and then stopped short.

"Because what?" I asked quickly.

Will put his hand on my shoulder.

"Shut up a minute, old man," he said in a low voice. "Let me tackle him."

He leaned more over the rail.

"See here, mister," he said, "this is a pretty queer business, you coming upon us like this, right out in the middle of the blessed Pacific. How are we to know what sort of a hanky-panky trick you're up to? You say there's only one of you. How are we to know, unless we get a squint at you—eh? What's your objection to the light, anyway?"

As he finished, I heard the noise of the oars again, and then the voice came, but now from a greater distance and sounding extremely hopeless and pathetic.

"I am sorry—sorry! I would not have troubled you, only I am hungry, and—so is she."

The voice died away, and the sound of the oars, dipping irregularly, was borne to us.

"Stop!" sung out Will. "I don't want to drive you away. Come back! We'll keep the light hidden if you don't like it."

He turned to me.

"It's a damned queer rig, this, but I think there's nothing to be afraid of."

There was a question in his tone, and I replied, "No, I think the poor devil's been wrecked around here and gone crazy."

The sound of the oars drew nearer.

"Shove that lamp back in the binnacle," said Will. Then he leaned over the rail and listened. I replaced the lamp and came back to his side. The dipping of the oars ceased some dozen yards distant.

"Won't you come alongside now?" asked Will in an even voice. "I have had the lamp put back in the binnacle."

"I—I cannot," replied the voice. "I dare not come

nearer. I dare not even pay you for the—the pro-visions."

"That's all right," said Will and hesitated. "You're welcome to as much grub as you can take." Again he hesitated.

"You are very good," exclaimed the voice. "May God, who understands everything, reward you—" It broke off huskily.

"The—the lady?" said Will abruptly. "Is she—?"

"I have left her behind upon the island," came the voice.

"What island?" I cut in.

"I know not its name," returned the voice. "I would to God—!" it began, and checked itself as suddenly.

"Could we not send a boat for her?" asked Will at this point.

"No!" said the voice with extraordinary emphasis. "My God! No!" There was a moment's pause; then it added, in a tone which seemed a merited reproach: "It was because of our want I ventured—because her agony tortured me."

"I am a forgetful brute," exclaimed Will. "Just wait a minute, whoever you are, and I will bring you up something at once."

In a couple of minutes he was back again, and his arms were full of various edibles. He paused at the rail.

"Can't you come alongside for them?" he asked.

"No—I *dare not*," replied the voice, and it seemed to me that in its tones I detected a note of stifled craving—as though the owner hushed a mortal desire. It came to me then in a flash that the poor old creature out there in the darkness was *suffering* for actual need of that which Will held in his arms, and yet, because of some unintelligible dread, refraining from dashing to the side of our little schooner and receiving it. And with the lightning-like conviction, there came the knowledge that the Invisible was not mad, but sanely facing some intolerable horror.

"Damn it, Will!" I said, full of many feelings over which predominated a vast sympathy. "Get a box. We must float off the stuff to him in it."

This we did, propelling it away from the vessel out into the darkness by means of a boat hook. In a minute a slight cry from the Invisible came to us, and we knew that he had secured the box.

A little later he called out a farewell to us and so heartful a blessing that I am sure we were the better for it. Then, without more ado, we heard the ply of oars across the darkness.

"Pretty soon off," remarked Will, with perhaps just a little sense of injury.

"Wait," I replied. "I think somehow he'll come back. He must have been badly needing that food."

"And the lady," said Will. For a moment he was silent; then he continued: "It's the queerest thing ever I've tumbled across since I've been fishing."

"Yes," I said and fell to pondering.

And so the time slipped away—an hour, another, and still Will stayed with me, for the queer adventure had knocked all desire for sleep out of him.

The third hour was three parts through when we heard again the sound of oars across the silent ocean.

"Listen!" said Will, a low note of excitement in his voice.

"He's coming, just as I thought," I muttered.

The dipping of the oars grew nearer, and I noted that the strokes were firmer and longer. The food had been needed.

They came to a stop a little distance off the broadside, and the queer voice came again to us through the darkness: "Schooner, ahoy!"

"That you?" asked Will.

"Yes," replied the voice. "I left you suddenly, but —but there was great need."

"The lady?" questioned Will.

"The—lady is grateful now on earth. She will be more grateful soon in—in heaven."

Will began to make some reply in a puzzled voice, but became confused and broke off short. I said nothing. I was wondering at the curious pauses, and, apart from my wonder, I was full of sympathy.

The voice continued: "We—she and I—have talked, as we shared the result of God's tenderness and yours—"

Will interposed, but without coherence.

"I beg of you not to—to belittle your deed of Christian charity this night," said the voice. "Be sure that it has not escaped His notice."

It stopped, and there was a full minute's silence. Then it came again.

"We have spoken together upon that which—which has befallen us. We had thought to go out without telling any of the terror which has come into our—lives. She is with me in believing that tonight's happenings are under a special ruling, and that it is God's wish that we should tell to you all that we have suffered since—since—"

"Yes?" said Will softly.

"Since the sinking of the *Albatross*."

"Ah!" I exclaimed involuntarily. "She left Newcastle for 'Frisco some six months ago, and hasn't been heard of since."

"Yes," answered the voice. "But some few degrees to the north of the line she was caught in a terrible storm and dismasted. When the day came it was found that she was leaking badly, and presently, it falling to a calm, the sailors took to the boats, leaving—leaving a young lady—my fiancée—and myself upon the wreck.

"We were below, gathering together a few of our belongings, when they left. They were entirely callous through fear, and when we came up upon the decks we saw them only as small shapes afar off upon the horizon. Yet we did not despair, but set to work and constructed a small raft. Upon this we put such few matters as it would hold, including a quantity of water and some ship's biscuit. Then, the vessel being very deep in the water, we got ourselves onto the raft and pushed off.

"It was later when I observed that we seemed to be in the way of some tide or current which bore us from the ship at an angle, so that in the course of three hours by my watch, her hull became invisible to our sight, her broken masts remaining in view for a somewhat longer period. Then, toward evening, it grew misty, and so through the night. The next day we were still encompassed by the mist, the weather remaining quiet.

"For four days we drifted through this strange haze until, on the evening of the fourth day, there grew upon our ears the murmur of breakers at a distance. Gradually it became plainer, and somewhat after midnight it appeared to sound upon either hand at no very great space. The raft was raised upon a swell several times, and then we were in smooth water and the noise of the breakers was behind.

"When the morning came we found that we were in a sort of great lagoon; but of this we noticed little at the time, for close before us, through the enshrouding mist, loomed the hull of a large sailing vessel. With one accord we fell upon our knees and thanked God, for we thought that here was an end to our perils. We had much to learn.

"The raft drew near to the ship and we shouted to them to take us aboard, but none answered. Presently the raft touched against the side of the vessel, and, seeing a rope hanging downward, I seized it and began to climb. Yet I had much ado to make my way up because of a kind of gray, lichenous fungus which had seized upon the rope and which blotched the side of the ship lividly.

"I reached the rail and clambered over it onto the deck. Here I saw that the decks were covered in great patches with the gray masses, some of them rising into nodules several feet in height, but at the time I thought less of this matter than of the possibility of there being people aboard the ship. I shouted, but none answered. Then I went to the door below the poop deck. I opened it and peered in. There was a great smell of staleness, so that I knew in a moment that nothing living was within, and with the knowledge I shut the door quickly, for I felt suddenly lonely.

"I went back to the side where I had scrambled up. My—my sweetheart was still sitting quietly upon the raft. Seeing me look down, she called up to know whether there were any aboard of the ship. I replied that the vessel had the appearance of having been long deserted, but that if she would wait a little I would see whether there was anything in the shape of a ladder by which she could ascend to the deck. Then we would make a search through the vessel together. A little later, on the opposite side of the decks, I found a rope side ladder. This I carried across, and a minute afterward she was beside me.

"Together we explored the cabins and apartments in the after part of the ship, but nowhere was there any sign of life. Here and there, within the cabins themselves, we came across odd patches of that queer fungus, but this, as my sweetheart said, could be cleansed away.

"In the end, having assured ourselves that the

after portion of the vessel was empty, we picked our ways to the bows between the ugly gray nodules of that strange growth. Here we made a further search, which told us that there was indeed none aboard but ourselves.

"This being now beyond any doubt, we returned to the stern of the ship and proceeded to make ourselves as comfortable as possible. Together we cleared out and cleaned two of the cabins, and after I made examination whether there was anything eatable in the ship. This I soon found was so and thanked God in my heart for His goodness. In addition to this I discovered the whereabouts of the freshwater pump, and, having fixed it, I found the water drinkable, though somewhat unpleasant to the taste.

"For several days we stayed aboard the ship without attempting to get to the shore. We were busily engaged in making the place habitable. Yet even this early we became aware that our lot was even less to be desired than might have been imagined, for though, as a first step, we scraped away the odd patches of growth that studded the floors and walls of the cabins and saloon, yet they returned almost to their original size within the space of twenty-four hours, which not only discouraged us, but gave us a feeling of vague unease.

"Still we would not admit ourselves beaten, so set to work afresh, and not only scraped away the fungus, but soaked the places where it had been with carbolic, a canful of which I had found in the pantry. Yet, by the end of the week the growth had returned in full strength, and in addition it had spread to other places, as though our touching it had allowed germs from it to travel elsewhere.

"On the seventh morning my sweetheart woke to find a small patch of it growing on her pillow close to her face. At that, she came to me, as soon as she could get her garments upon her. I was in the galley at the time lighting the fire for breakfast.

"'Come here, John,' she said and led me aft. When I saw the thing upon her pillow I shuddered, and then and there we agreed to go right out of the ship and see whether we could not fare to make ourselves more comfortable ashore.

"Hurriedly we gathered together our few belongings, and even among these I found that the fungus had been at work, for one of her shawls had a little lump of it growing near one edge. I threw the whole thing over the side without saying anything to her.

"The raft was still alongside, but it was too clumsy to guide, and I lowered down a small boat that hung across the stern, and in this we made our way to the shore. Yet, as we drew near to it, I became gradually aware that here the vile fungus which had driven us from the ship was growing riot. In places it rose into horrible, fantastic mounds which seemed almost to quiver as with a quiet life when the wind blew across them. Here and there it took on the forms of vast fingers, and in others it just spread out flat and smooth and treacherous. Odd places, it appeared as grotesque, stunted trees, seeming extraordinarily kinked and gnarled—the whole quaking vilely at times.

"At first it seemed to us that there was no single portion of the surrounding shore which was not hidden beneath the masses of the hideous lichen; yet in this I found we were mistaken, for somewhat later, coasting along the shore at a little distance, we descried a smooth white patch of what appeared to be fine sand, and there we landed. It was not sand. What it was I do not know. All that I have observed is that upon it the fungus will not grow, while every-where else, save where the sandlike earth wanders oddly pathwise amid the gray desolation of the lichen, there is nothing but that loathsome grayness.

"It is difficult to make you understand how cheered we were to find one place that was absolutely free from the growth, and here we deposited our belong-ings. Then we went back to the ship for such things as it seemed to us we should need. Among other matters, I managed to bring ashore with me one of the ship's sails, with which I constructed two small tents, which, though exceedingly rough-shaped, served the purposes for which they were intended. In these we lived and stored our various necessities, and thus for a matter of some four weeks all went smoothly and without particular unhappiness. In-deed, I may say with much of happiness—for—for we were together.

"It was on the thumb of her right hand that the growth first showed. It was only a small circular spot, much like a little gray mole. My God! how the fear leapt to my heart when she showed me the place. We cleansed it, between us, washing it with carbolic and water. In the morning of the following day she showed her hand to me again. The gray warty thing had returned. For a little while we looked at one another in silence. Then, still wordless, we started again to remove it. In the midst of the operation she spoke suddenly.

" 'What's that on the side of your face, dear?' Her voice was sharp with anxiety. I put my hand up to feel.

" 'There! Under the hair by your ear. A little to the front a bit.' My finger rested upon the place, and then I knew.

" 'Let us get your thumb done first,' I said. And she submitted, only because she was afraid to touch me until it was cleansed. I finished washing and disinfecting her thumb, and then she turned to my face. After it was finished we sat together and talked awhile of many things, for there had come into our lives sudden, very terrible thoughts. We were all at once afraid of something worse than death. We spoke of loading the boat with provisions and water and making our way out to the sea; yet we were helpless, for many causes, and—and the growth had attacked us already. We decided to stay. God would do with us what was His will. We would wait.

"A month, two months, three months passed and the places grew somewhat, and there had come others. Yet we fought so strenuously with the fear that its headway was slow, comparatively speaking.

"Occasionally we ventured off to the ship for such stores as we needed. There we found that the fungus grew persistently. One of the nodules on the main deck soon became as high as my head.

"We had now given up all thought or hope of leaving the island. We had realized that it would be unallowable to go among healthy humans with the things from which we were suffering.

"With this determination and knowledge in our minds we knew that we should have to husband our food and water, for we did not know at that time but we should possibly live for many years.

"This reminds me that I have told you that I am an old man. Judged by years this is not so. But— but—" He broke off, then continued somewhat abruptly: "As I was saying, we knew that we should have to use care in the matter of food. But we had no idea then how little food there was left, of which to take care. It was a week later that I made the discovery that all the other bread tanks—which I had supposed full—were empty, and that (beyond odd tins of vegetables and meat and some other matters) we had nothing on which to depend but the bread in the tank which I had already opened.

"After learning this I bestirred myself to do what I could and set to work at fishing in the lagoon, but with no success. At this I was somewhat inclined to feel desperate until the thought came to me to try outside the lagoon, in the open sea.

"Here, at times, I caught odd fish, but so infrequently that they proved of but little help in keeping us from the hunger which threatened. It seemed to me that our deaths were likely to come by hunger and not by the growth of the thing which had seized upon our bodies.

"We were in this state of mind when the fourth month wore out. Then I made a very horrible discovery. One morning, a little before midday, I came off from the ship with a portion of the biscuits which were left. In the mouth of her tent I saw my sweetheart sitting, eating something.

" 'What is it, my dear?' I called out as I leapt ashore. Yet, on hearing my voice, she seemed confused and, turning, slyly threw something toward the edge of the little clearing. It fell short, and a vague suspicion having arisen within me, I walked across and picked it up. It was a piece of the gray fungus.

"As I went to her with it in my hand she turned deadly pale, then a rose red.

"I felt strangely dazed and frightened.

" 'My dear! My dear!' I said and could say no more. Yet at my words she broke down and cried bitterly. Gradually, as she calmed, I got from her the news that she had tried it the preceding day and —and liked it. I got her to promise on her knees not to touch it again, however great our hunger. After she had promised she told me that the desire for it had come suddenly, and that until the moment of desire she had experienced nothing toward it but the most extreme repulsion.

"Later in the day, feeling strangely restless and much shaken with the thing which I had discovered,

I made my way along one of the twisted paths—
formed by the white, sandlike substance—which
led among the fungoid growth. I had once before
ventured along there, but not to any great distance.
This time, being involved in perplexing thought, I
went much farther than hitherto.

"Suddenly I was called to myself by a queer hoarse
sound on my left. Turning quickly, I saw that there
was movement among an extraordinarily shaped mass
of fungus close to my elbow. It was swaying uneasily,
as though it possessed life of its own. Abruptly, as I
stared, the thought came to me that the thing had
a grotesque resemblance to the figure of a distorted
human creature. Even as the fancy flashed into my
brain, there was a slight, sickening noise of tearing,
and I saw that one of the branchlike arms was
detaching itself from the surrounding gray masses
and coming toward me. The head of the thing—a
shapeless gray ball—inclined in my direction. I stood
stupidly, and the vile arm brushed across my face.
I gave out a frightened cry and ran back a few
paces. There was a sweetish taste upon my lips where
the thing had touched me. I licked them and was
immediately filled with an inhuman desire. I turned
and seized a mass of the fungus—then more and more.
I was insatiable. In the midst of devouring, the remembrance of the morning's discovery swept into
my mazed brain. It was sent by God. I dashed the
fragment I held to the ground. Then, utterly wretched
and feeling a dreadful guiltiness, I made my way
back to the little encampment.

"I think she knew, by some marvelous intuition which love must have given, as soon as she set eyes on me. Her quiet sympathy made it easier for me, and I told her of my sudden weakness, yet omitted to mention the extraordinary thing which had gone before. I desired to spare her all unnecessary terror.

"But, for myself, I had added an intolerable knowledge, to breed an incessant terror in my brain, for I doubted not but that I had seen the end of one of those men who had come to the island in the ship in the lagoon, and in that monstrous ending I had seen our own.

"Thereafter we kept from the abominable food, though the desire for it had entered into our blood. Yet our drear punishment was upon us, for day by day, with monstrous rapidity, the fungoid growth took hold of our poor bodies. Nothing we could do would check it materially, and so—and so—we who had been human became— Well, it matters less each day. Only—only we had been man and maid!

"And day by day the fight is more dreadful to withstand the hunger-lust for the terrible lichen.

"A week ago we ate the last of the biscuit, and since that time I have caught three fish. I was out here fishing tonight when your schooner drifted upon me out of the mist. I hailed you. You know the rest, and may God, out of His great heart, bless you for your goodness to a—a couple of poor outcast souls."

There was the dip of an oar—another. Then the voice came again, and for the last time, sounding through the slight surrounding mist, ghostly and mournful.

"God bless you! Good-bye."

"Good-bye," we shouted together hoarsely, our hearts full of many emotions.

I glanced about me. I became aware that the dawn was upon us.

The sun flung a stray beam across the hidden sea, pierced the mist dully, and lit up the receding boat with a gloomy fire. Indistinctly I saw something nodding between the oars. I thought of a sponge—a great, gray, nodding sponge. The oars continued to ply. They were gray—as was the boat—and my eyes searched a moment vainly for the conjunction of hand and oar. My gaze flashed back to the head. It nodded forward as the oars went backward for the stroke. Then the oars were dipped, the boat shot out of the patch of light, and the—the thing went nodding into the mist.

The Extra Passenger

August Derleth

Mr. Arodias had worked a long time on his plan to kill his eccentric uncle, and he was very proud of it. But then, Mr. Arodias was a very clever man; he had lived by his wits for so many years that it had never been necessary for him to kill Uncle Thaddeus before. Only now that Mr. Arodias was getting along toward middle age, and his fingers were no longer so nimble as they had once been, the time came. He began by thinking that he ought not to be deprived of his inheritance any longer and ended up by working out the perfect crime, which he defied Scotland Yard to solve.

Like all such plans, it was almost absurdly simple, and Mr. Arodias indulged in many a self-congratulatory chuckle when he contemplated the bumbling efforts of the CID to solve it. Uncle Thaddeus, who was a recluse, lived on the edge of Sudbury, which was on the Aberdeen line from London. Three squares from his tree-girt house lived another solitary who owned a fast car and kept it carelessly in an unlocked shed some distance from his house. Thirty miles from Sudbury, where the night train to

Aberdeen stopped, lay the hamlet of East Chelmly, the next stop, rather in a curving line from Sudbury, so that it was farther by rail than by highway. It would be a simple matter to take off for Aberdeen from London on the slow night train, slip out of his compartment at Sudbury, "take care" of Uncle Thaddeus, then appropriate his neighbor's fast car, and arrive in East Chelmly in adequate time to slip back onto his train, with none the wiser. A perfect alibi! Ah, what chuckleheads he would make of the laddies from the Yard!

Moreover, it worked like a charm. True, the old man had recognized him and had muttered something about coming after him before the light in his crafty eyes went out and his battered head fell forward—but it was just a matter of moments; the whole thing had been rehearsed in Mr. Arodias' mind so often that he knew just what to do and flattered himself by thinking that he could have done it blindfolded. The old dodderer nearby had left his car plentifully supplied with petrol, too, as if he had been an accomplice, and it took Mr. Arodias to East Chelmly in the dead of night, never meeting anyone on the long road, never seeing anyone in the little hamlets through which he passed. He arrived in East Chelmly in excellent time, and like a shadow he slipped around to the station and into his compartment with no one seeing.

No one, that is, except the extra passenger.

For at this point in his perfect crime Mr. Arodias came face-to-face with a factor for which he had made no provision. He had left his compartment empty, save for his bags and golf clubs; he came back to it to find huddled in the opposite seat, with his hat well down over his face, an extra passenger. It was possible that the fellow had not marked Mr. Arodias' entrance, but, much to his annoyance, Mr. Arodias could not be sure.

"Sorry to disturb you," he said genially. "I have been in the lavatory."

No answer.

Mr. Arodias hawked once or twice.

No sign of life.

Mr. Arodias settled back, relieved, feeling very comfortable and secure. This pleasant feeling of security did not last, however. In a few moments he was asking himself where in the devil the extra passenger had come from. There had been no stop between Sudbury and East Chelmly. The compartment was in one of the through coaches, not a local. It was barely possible that a passenger from one of the other compartments had mistaken Mr. Arodias' for his own in the dark and now occupied it by mistake. For it was still dark, being somewhat past midnight, and the lights in the corridor were dim.

But this explanation did not satisfy Mr. Arodias, and he was possessed of a normal dislike of unsatisfactory matters. This was all the more true when the matter in question represented a potential flaw in what he felt was a very perfect plan. His fellow traveler, however, was apparently oblivious of his growing perturbation; he continued to huddle there without movement other than that caused by the train rushing through the night. This troubled Mr. Arodias; he expected nothing less than a full account explaining the extra passenger's presence.

Failing this, he began to imagine all kinds of things, and he took every opportunity to examine his companion in the light of passing stations. He wore heavy, almost loutish shoes. Obviously a countryman. His hands, which did not seem clean, were those of an old man. His hat had seen much roughing. Of his face, Mr. Arodias saw nothing. How long, he wondered, had he been sleeping? If he had just simply blundered into the compartment and settled down and dozed right off, all would be well. But if he had not done so, he might well be in a position to ask annoying questions about what kept Mr. Arodias in the lavatory for time enough to enable the train to put close to sixty or seventy miles behind from the time he had entered the lavatory—which was, of course, presumably at the same hour the extra passenger had entered Mr. Arodias' compartment.

This thought needled Mr. Arodias with desperation. Already he had visions of some officious bumpkin plodding to the police station in Aberdeen and solemnly deposing that Mr. Arodias' late entrance was a suspicious circumstance. He could see it in cold print. *"Sudbury Victim's Heir Questioned,"* the headline would read. And this unwelcome stranger, huddled there like a tangible threat to his security, would have put all his suspicions down. " 'E come late into 'is seat, an' I could na 'elp wonderin' where

the zur kep' 'imself all that time. A good hour, 't was. Nor did 'e 'ave the look of a zick man about 'im."

Mr. Arodias could hardly contain himself. He coughed loudly. Fancying that he saw a movement about his fellow traveler not inspired by the train, he said hastily, "Forgive me. I didn't mean to awaken you."

But there was no answer.

Mr. Arodias bit his lip. "I say," he said firmly.

Silence.

The sounds of the train filled the compartment— the whistle up ahead, the rush of steam, the clicking of the drivers—filled the room and rolled around in it, swelling and growing. It was grotesque. It made such a sound that it would have awakened the dead, thought Mr. Arodias. Yet the extra passenger slept calmly through it, huddled there like someone lost in the deepest dream.

He leaned forward and tapped the fellow on the knee.

"Look here, this is my compartment, you know."

No answer.

Oh, it was maddening! Especially so for a man of Mr. Arodias' temperament, and most particularly since this was happening just after he had brought off what was certain to come out in the end as his most successful coup in a career of successes. This confounded extra passenger was by his very presence, however innocuous he might be, taking the edge of enjoyment off his pleasure in his accomplishment of that night.

Mr. Arodias considered shaking the fellow.

But this he dismissed from his mind within a few moments. There was, after all, no good antagonizing him. There was no reason to believe that he had seen a single thing which might make him suspicious. Indeed, he might leave the compartment at any place along the line without once realizing that he sat in the same train with the heir to the Sudbury recluse. No, there was absolutely no good in unnecessarily attracting attention to himself.

He felt frustrated, and he redoubled his efforts to examine his fellow traveler. He took the trouble, finally, to take out his pipe, fill it, and strike a match, rather more for the purpose of examining the extra passenger in its flickering light than for that of lighting his pipe. Then for the first time he observed that the fellow had no baggage of any kind. Manifestly, then, he had stumbled into the wrong compartment. The shoes were country shoes, all right. Clodhopperish. Mud on them, too. And on his hands. Uncouth fellow.

Or was it mud? The match went out.

Mr. Arodias was afraid to light another. For one cataclysmic moment the stuff on his fellow traveler's hands and shoes had looked like blood! Mr. Arodias swallowed and told himself that he was having hallucinations stemming from some rudimentary conscience which had not died with the rest of it in that long-ago time when he had entered upon his life of dubious practices and crime.

He sat for a long moment in silence. The hour

was now past two in the morning. He busied himself for a little while peering out of the window,
trying to ascertain just where the train was at the
moment. Approaching the Scottish border, he decided. He closed his eyes and tried to think how he
must act when they found him in Aberdeen and told
him his Uncle Thaddeus was dead, slain by an
unknown assailant in the night, while he was on his
way to Scotland under the protection of such a perfect alibi. But there was nothing to be gained in
thinking about this; he had decided upon his course
of action right up to the moment he actually took
possession of his inheritance—he had decided upon
that long ago; it was all an integral part of his plan.
Indeed, the only incident which was not integral in
his plan was this extra passenger.

He turned to him again, hawked once more,
coughed loudly, knocked his pipe out on the window-
sill, and looked hopefully over through the darkness
of the compartment at that huddled old fellow in the
corner of his seat.

No movement.

"This has gone far enough," he said aloud, becoming vexed.

Silence.

He leaned over once more and tapped his companion on the knee with some persistence. "Look
here, you're in the wrong compartment, sir."

This time he got an answer. It was a muttered,
sleepy "No."

The voice was guttural, broken. Mr. Arodias was

slightly disconcerted but in one way relieved.

"I'm sorry," he said in a more pleasant tone, "but I believe you got into my compartment by mistake."

"No," said his companion again.

Instantly annoyed once more, Mr. Arodias wondered why the fellow insisted on talking from beneath his hat.

"Where did you get on the train?" he asked with some asperity.

"In Sudbury."

Sudbury! Of course! That could have been. Why had he not thought of that? He had been in such a hurry to get off the train he had not thought that someone might get on. He was about to speak again when his companion added a catastrophic afterthought.

"Where you got off," he said.

After but a moment of cold shock, Mr. Arodias rallied. "Yes, I stepped out for a breath of air and then went to the lavatory when I got back."

"I thought," the old man went on with a burr of dialect in his voice, just as Mr. Arodias had imagined, "you might have gone to see your uncle."

Mr. Arodias sat quite still. Faced with this challenge, his mind worked with the speed of lightning. Within ten seconds Mr. Arodias decided that, whoever he was, the extra passenger must never leave the night train alive. He might know nothing at all of the crime, but he nevertheless knew enough to hang Mr. Arodias. He knew enough, indeed; he knew Mr. Arodias, he knew he had got off at Sudbury, and no doubt he knew he had reappeared in his compartment in the vicinity of East Chelmly. That was enough to doom one of them, and Mr. Arodias, having got this far, had no intention of being doomed.

Mr. Arodias needed time, and he was now quite willing to spar for it until he had evolved a plan for eliminating this menacing old fellow and dumping his body somewhere along the right-of-way.

"You know my uncle?" he asked in a strained voice.

"Aye, quite well."

"I don't know him too well myself. I'm a Londoner, and he keeps to his own place in the country."

"Aye. He has reasons, you might say."

Mr. Arodias pricked up his ears. "What reasons?" he asked bluntly.

"A pity you don't know."

"I don't," said Mr. Arodias, irritated.

"A pity you didn't know a bit more."

"If there's something about my uncle I ought to know, I would like to hear it."

"Aye, you shall. Your uncle's a mage."

"A mage?" Mr. Arodias was mystified.

"A warlock, then, if you like that better."

Mr. Arodias was amazed. He was also touched with a kind of macabre amusement. He did not know why the fact that the old man's fellow villagers regarded him as a warlock should amuse him, yet it did. Even in his amusement he did not lose sight of his decision that this prying oldster must die, and he was contemplating whether he should dispatch him with a quick blow or two or whether he should stifle his outcries and strangle him. The important thing, of course, was to prevent the guard from hearing anything suspicious. Meanwhile he must carry on. Best to humor the extra passenger.

"Warlock, eh? And no doubt he has some special talents?" He caught himself just in time to prevent his saying "had"; it would never do to refer to Uncle Thaddeus in the past tense—just in case something went wrong and his curious fellow traveler got away after all.

"Aye, that he had."

"Foretold the weather, no doubt."

"That any gibbering fool could do."

"Told fortunes, then?"

"A gypsy's trade! Not he! But then, you always did underrate him."

"Did I, now?"

"Aye."

"What was so wonderful about his being a warlock—if he was."

"Oh, he was. Never a doubt about that. He had his familiar, too—on wings."

"Wings?"

"Aye. He brought me to the train."

Mr. Arodias looked askance. A kind of premonitory tingle crept up his spine. He blinked and wished the light were a little stronger. There was beginning to be something uncomfortably challenging about his chosen victim; Mr. Arodias did not like it.

"And he could send about a lich or two, if he had a mind to."

"A lich?" said Mr. Arodias in a dry voice. "What the devil's that?"

"You don't know?"

"I wouldn't ask you if I did."

"It's a corpse, that's what."

"Send it about? What are you talking about?" demanded Mr. Arodias, feeling a chill along his arms.

"Aye—for a special purpose. Oh, your uncle was a great one for things like that."

"Special purpose," repeated Mr. Arodias, and at that moment his foot touched upon a sturdy weight which had the feel of a sash weight, and he bent to take it in his hand. Yes, it would do; it would do very well; and it was getting to be high time that he used it, because there was something horrible and terrible about that huddled figure.

"A special purpose," said the extra passenger. "Like this one."

Mr. Arodias was suddenly aware that his traveling companion had been speaking of his uncle for the past few minutes in the past tense. A kind of constriction seized upon his throat; but his fingers tightened upon the weight in his hand. The extra passenger knew or guessed far too much; whatever the risk, he must die now—quickly. He leaned forward stealthily, as if he thought that the old fellow could see him despite the darkness and the hat over his face.

Then he snatched the hat away and aimed his first blow.

It did not fall.

The head under that hat was hardly half a head—

smashed in and with the blood run down all over the face—the head of his Uncle Thaddeus! A scream rose and died in Mr. Arodias' throat.

The eyes in that battered head were looking at him, and they were shining as if lit by the fires of hell.

No word, no sound passed Mr. Arodias' lips; he was incapable of speech, of movement. A power, a force beyond Mr. Arodias' comprehension emanated from the thing on the seat opposite. The eyes held him, the eyes encompassed him, the eyes drew him. Mr. Arodias shrank together and slipped from the seat to his knees on the floor of the compartment. As in a dream he heard the sounds of the train, coming as if from very far away.

"Come to me, Simon," said the thing that had been his Uncle Thaddeus.

And Simon Arodias crept across the floor and groveled.

"Bring your face closer, Simon."

And Simon Arodias raised his head, with a harsh whimpering sound struggling for utterance in his throat. Powerless to move, he watched one of the thick, bloody hands of the extra passenger come down like a vise upon his face. Then he saw nothing more and heard the sound of the night train like the sound of doom thundering in his ears.

The guard who found Mr. Arodias collapsed from shock.

The medical examiner at Aberdeen was upset for

a week. Nevertheless, despite the condition of Mr. Arodias' face—what was left of it—it was ascertained that he had been suffocated—"by person or persons unknown." Circumstances notwithstanding, Mr. Arodias could not have committed suicide.

As for those fumbling chuckleheads at Scotland Yard—they had already found the gloves which Mr. Arodias had discarded on his way from the stolen car abandoned in East Chelmly to the station, the gloves which were to lead them all in good time to the little plot of ground where Mr. Arodias was enjoying, not his Uncle Thaddeus' money, but his own just due.

Casting the Runes

M. R. James

April 15, 190—

DEAR SIR:

I am requested by the Council of the ____ Association to return to you the draft of a paper on *The Truth of Alchemy*, which you have been good enough to offer to read at our forthcoming meeting, and to inform you that the council do not see their way to including it in the program.

I am,

Yours faithfully,

____, SECRETARY

April 18

DEAR SIR:

I am sorry to say that my engagements do not permit of my affording you an interview on the subject of your proposed paper. Nor do our laws allow of your discussing the matter with a committee of our council, as you suggest. Please allow me to assure you that the fullest consideration was given to the draft which you submitted, and that it was not declined without having been referred to the judgment of a most competent authority. No personal question (it can hardly be necessary for me to add) can have had the slightest influence on the decision of the council.

Believe me (ut supra)

April 20

The Secretary of the _____ Association begs respectfully to inform Mr. Karswell that it is impossible for him to communicate the name of any person or persons to whom the draft of Mr. Karswell's paper may have been submitted, and further desires to intimate that he cannot undertake to reply to any further letters on this subject.

"And who *is* Mr. Karswell?" inquired the Secretary's wife. She had called at his office and (perhaps unwarrantably) had picked up the last of these three letters, which the typist had just brought in.

"Why, my dear, just at present Mr. Karswell is a very angry man. But I don't know much about him otherwise, except that he is a person of wealth, his address is Lufford Abbey, Warwickshire, and he's an alchemist, apparently, and wants to tell us all about it; and that's about all—except that I don't want to meet him for the next week or two. Now, if you're ready to leave this place, I am."

"What have you been doing to make him angry?" asked Mrs. Secretary.

"The usual thing, my dear, the usual thing. He sent in a draft of a paper he wanted to read at the next meeting, and we referred it to Edward Dunning —almost the only man in England who knows about these things—and he said it was perfectly hopeless, so we declined it. So Karswell has been pelting me with letters ever since. The last thing he wanted was the name of the man we referred his nonsense to; you saw my answer to that. But don't you say anything about it, for goodness' sake."

"I should think not, indeed. Did I ever do such a thing? I do hope, though, he won't get to know that it was poor Mr. Dunning."

"Poor Mr. Dunning? I don't know why you call him that; he's a very happy man, is Dunning. Lots of hobbies and a comfortable home and all his time to himself."

"I only meant I should be sorry for him if this man got hold of his name and came and bothered him."

"Oh, ah! yes. I daresay he would be poor Mr. Dunning then."

The Secretary and his wife were lunching out, and the friends to whose house they were bound were Warwickshire people. So Mrs. Secretary had already settled it in her own mind that she would question them judiciously about Mr. Karswell. But she was saved the trouble of leading up to the subject, for the hostess said to the host, before many minutes had passed, "I saw the Abbot of Lufford this morning." The host whistled. "*Did* you? What in the world brings him up to town?" "Goodness knows; he was coming out of the British Museum gate as I drove past." It was not unnatural that Mrs. Secretary should inquire whether this was a real abbot who was being spoken of. "Oh, no, my dear, only a neighbor of ours in the country who bought Lufford Abbey a few years ago. His real name is Karswell." "Is he a friend of yours?" asked Mr. Secretary, with a private wink to his wife. The question let loose a torrent of declamation. There was really nothing to be said for Mr. Karswell. Nobody knew what he did with himself; his servants were a horrible set of people; he had invented a new religion for himself, and practiced no one could tell what appalling rites; he was very easily offended, and never forgave anybody; he had a dreadful face (so the lady insisted, her husband somewhat demurring); he never did a kind action, and whatever influence he did exert was mischievous. "Do the poor man justice, dear," the husband interrupted. "You forget the treat he gave the schoolchildren." "Forget it, indeed! But I'm glad you mentioned it, because it gives an idea of the man. Now, Florence, listen to this. The first winter he was at Lufford this delightful neighbor of ours wrote to the clergyman of his parish (he's not ours, but we know him very well) and offered to show the schoolchildren some magic lantern slides. He said he had some new kinds which he thought would interest them. Well, the clergyman was rather surprised because Mr. Karswell had shown himself inclined to be unpleasant to the children—complaining of their trespassing or something of the sort— but of course he accepted, and the evening was fixed, and our friend went himself to see that everything

went right. He said he never had been so thankful
for anything as that his own children were all prevented from being there—they were at a children's
party at our house, as a matter of fact. Because this
Mr. Karswell had evidently set out with the intention of frightening these poor village children out
of their wits, and I do believe if he had been allowed
to go on he would actually have done so. He began
with some comparatively mild things. Red Riding
Hood was one, and even then, Mr. Farrer said, the
wolf was so dreadful that several of the smaller
children had to be taken out, and he said Mr. Karswell began the story by producing a noise like a
wolf howling in the distance, which was the most
gruesome thing he had ever heard. All the slides
he showed, Mr. Farrer said, were most clever; they
were absolutely realistic, and where he had got them
or how he worked them he could not imagine. Well,
the show went on, and the stories kept on becoming
a little more terrifying each time, and the children
were mesmerized into complete silence. At last he
produced a series which represented a little boy
passing through his own park—Lufford, I mean—in
the evening. Every child in the room could recognize
the place from the pictures. And this poor boy was
followed, and at last pursued and overtaken, and
either torn in pieces or somehow made away with
by a horrible hopping creature in white, which you
saw first dodging about among the trees, and gradually it appeared more and more plainly. Mr. Farrer
said it gave him one of the worst nightmares he ever

remembered, and what it must have meant to the children doesn't bear thinking of. Of course this was too much, and he spoke very sharply indeed to Mr. Karswell and said it couldn't go on. All *he* said was, 'Oh, you think it's time to bring our little show to an end and send them home to their beds? *Very* well!' And then, if you please, he switched on another slide, which showed a great mass of snakes, centipedes, and disgusting creatures with wings, and somehow or other he made it seem as if they were climbing out of the picture and getting in amongst the audience; and this was accompanied by a sort of dry, rustling noise which sent the children nearly mad, and of course they stampeded. A good many of them were rather hurt in getting out of the room, and I don't suppose one of them closed an eye that night. There was the most dreadful trouble in the village afterward. Of course the mothers threw a good part of the blame on poor Mr. Farrer, and if they could have got past the gates, I believe the fathers would have broken every window in the Abbey. Well, now, that's Mr. Karswell—that's the Abbot of Lufford, my dear, and you can imagine how we covet *his* society."

"Yes, I think he has all the possibilities of a distinguished criminal, has Karswell," said the host. "I should be sorry for anyone who got into his bad books."

"Is he the man, or am I mixing him up with someone else?" asked the Secretary (who for some minutes had been wearing the frown of the man who is trying to recollect something). "Is he the man who brought out a *History of Witchcraft* some time back—ten years or more?"

"That's the man; do you remember the reviews of it?"

"Certainly I do, and what's equally to the point, I knew the author of the most incisive of the lot. So did you. You must remember John Harrington; he was at John's in our time."

"Oh, very well indeed, though I don't think I saw or heard anything of him between the time I went down and the day I read the account of the inquest on him."

"Inquest?" said one of the ladies. "What happened to him?"

"Why, what happened was that he fell out of a tree and broke his neck. But the puzzle was what could have induced him to get up there. It was a mysterious business, I must say. Here was this man —not an athletic fellow, was he? and with no eccentric twist about him that was ever noticed—walking home along a country road late in the evening—no tramps about—well known and liked in the place— and he suddenly begins to run like mad, loses his hat and stick, and finally shins up a tree—quite a difficult tree—growing in the hedgerow. A dead branch gives way, and he comes down with it and breaks his neck, and there he's found next morning with the most dreadful face of fear on him that could be imagined. It was pretty evident, of course, that he had been chased by something, and people talked of savage dogs and beasts escaped out of menageries; but there was nothing to be made of that. That was in '89, and I believe his brother Henry (whom I remember as well at Cambridge, but you probably don't) has been trying to get on the track of an explanation ever since. He, of course, insists there was malice in it, but I don't know. It's difficult to see how it could have come in."

After a time the talk reverted to the *History of Witchcraft.*

"Did you ever look into it?" asked the host.

"Yes, I did," said the Secretary. "I went so far as to read it."

"Was it as bad as it was made out to be?"

"Oh, in point of style and form, quite hopeless. It deserved all the pulverizing it got. But, besides that, it was an evil book. The man believed every word of what he was saying, and I'm very much mistaken if he hadn't tried the greater part of his recipes."

"Well, I only remember Harrington's review of it, and I must say if I'd been the author it would have quenched my literary ambition for good. I should never have held up my head again."

"It hasn't had that effect in the present case. But come, it's half-past three; I must be off."

On the way home the Secretary's wife said, "I do hope that horrible man won't find out that Mr. Dunning had anything to do with the rejection of his paper."

"I don't think there's much chance of that," said the Secretary. "Dunning won't mention it himself, for these matters are confidential, and none of us will for the same reason. Karswell won't know his name, for Dunning hasn't published anything on the same subject yet. The only danger is that Karswell might find out, if he were to ask the British Museum people, who was in the habit of consulting alchemical manuscripts. I can't very well tell them not to mention Dunning, can I? It would set them talking at once. Let's hope it won't occur to him."

However, Mr. Karswell was an astute man.

This much is in the way of prologue. On an evening rather later in the same week, Mr. Edward Dunning was returning from the British Museum, where he had been engaged in research, to the comfortable house in a suburb where he lived alone, tended by two excellent women who had been long with him. There is nothing to be added by way of description of him to what we have heard already. Let us follow him as he takes his sober course homeward.

A train took him to within a mile or two of his house and an electric tram a stage farther. The line ended at a point some three hundred yards from his front door. He had had enough of reading when he got into the car, and indeed the light was not such as to allow him to do more than study the advertisements on the panes of glass that faced him as he sat. As was not unnatural, the advertisements in this particular line of cars were objects of his frequent contemplation, and, with the possible exception of the brilliant and convincing dialogue between Mr.

Lamplough and an eminent K.C. on the subject of Pyretic Saline, none of them afforded much scope to his imagination. I am wrong: there was one at the corner of the car farthest from him which did not seem familiar. It was in blue letters on a yellow ground, and all that he could read of it was a name— —John Harrington—and something like a date. It could be of no interest to him to know more, but for all that, as the car emptied, he was just curious enough to move along the seat until he could read it well. He felt to a slight extent repaid for his trouble; the advertisement was *not* of the usual type. It ran thus: "In memory of John Harrington, F.S.A., of The Laurels, Ashbrooke. Died Sept. 18, 1889. Three months were allowed."

The car stopped. Mr. Dunning, still contemplating the blue letters on the yellow ground, had to be stimulated to rise by a word from the conductor. "I beg your pardon," he said, "I was looking at that advertisement; it's a very odd one, isn't it?" The conductor read it slowly. "Well, my word," he said, "I never see that one before. Well, that is a cure, ain't it? Someone bin up to their jokes 'ere, I should think." He got out a duster and applied it, not without saliva, to the pane and then to the outside. "No," he said, returning, "that ain't no transfer; seems to me as if it was reg'lar *in* the glass—what I mean in the substance, as you may say. Don't you think so, sir?" Mr. Dunning examined it and rubbed it with his glove and agreed. "Who looks after these advertisements and gives leave for them to be put up? I wish

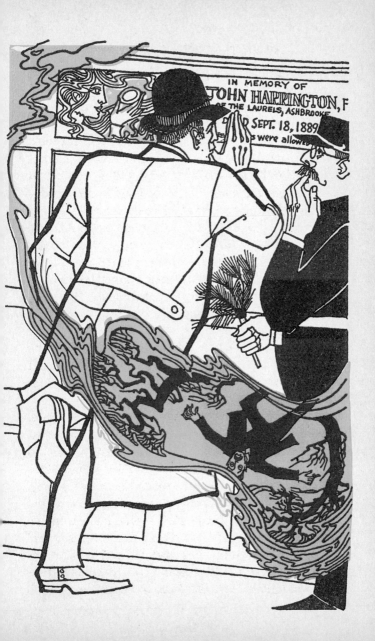

IN MEMORY OF
JOHN HARRINGTON, F
OF THE LAURELS, ASHBROOKE
SEPT. 18, 1889
were allowed

you would inquire. I will just take a note of the words." At this moment there came a call from the driver: "Look alive, George, time's up." "All right, all right; there's something else what's up at this end. You come and look at this 'ere glass." "What's gorn with the glass?" said the driver, approaching. "Well, and oo's 'Arrington? What's it all about?" "I was just asking who was responsible for putting the advertisements up in your cars and saying it would be as well to make some inquiry about this one." "Well, sir, that's all done at the company's orfice, that work is. It's our Mr. Timms, I believe, looks into that. When we put up tonight I'll leave word, and per'aps I'll be able to tell you tomorrer if you 'appen to be coming this way."

This was all that passed that evening. Mr. Dunning did just go to the trouble of looking up Ashbrooke and found that it was in Warwickshire.

Next day he went to town again. The car (it was the same car) was too full in the morning to allow of his getting a word with the conductor. He could only be sure that the curious advertisement had been made away with. The close of the day brought a further element of mystery into the transaction. He had missed the tram, or else preferred walking home, but at a rather late hour, while he was at work in his study, one of the maids came to say that two men from the tramways were very anxious to speak to him. This was a reminder of the advertisement, which he had, he says, nearly forgotten. He had the men in —they were the conductor and driver of the car—

and when the matter of refreshment had been attended to, asked what Mr. Timms had had to say about the advertisement.

"Well, sir, that's what we took the liberty to step round about," said the conductor. "Mr. Timms 'e give William 'ere the rough side of his tongue about that: 'cordin' to 'im there warn't no advertisement of that description sent in, nor ordered, nor paid for, nor put up, nor nothink, let alone not bein' there, and we was playing the fool takin' up his time. 'Well,' I says, 'if that's the case, all I ask of you, Mr. Timms,' I says, 'is to take and look at it for yourself,' I says. 'Of course, if it ain't there,' I says, 'you may take and call me what you like.' 'Right,' he says, 'I will.' And we went straight off. Now, I leave it to you, sir, if that ad, as we term 'em, with 'Arrington on it warn't as plain as ever you see anythink—blue letters on yeller glass, and as I says at the time, and you borne me out, reg'lar *in* the glass, because, if you remember, you recollect of me swabbing it off with my duster."

"To be sure I do, quite clearly—well?"

"You may say well, I don't think. Mr. Timms he gets in that car with a light—no, he told William to 'old the light outside. 'Now,' he says, 'where's your precious ad what we've 'eard so much about?' ' 'Ere it is,' I says, 'Mr. Timms,' and I laid my 'and on it." The conductor paused.

"Well," said Mr. Dunning, "it was gone, I suppose. Broken?"

"Broke!—not it. There warn't, if you'll believe me,

no more trace of them letters—blue letters they was
—on that piece o' glass, than—well, it's no good *me*
talkin'. *I* never see such a thing. I leave it to William
here if—but there, as I says, where's the benefit in
me going on about it?"

"And what did Mr. Timms say?"

"Why, 'e did what I give 'im leave to—called us
pretty much anythink he liked, and I don't know
as I blame him so much, neither. But what we
thought, William and me did, was as we seen you
take down a bit of a note about that—well, that
letterin'. . . ."

"I certainly did that, and I have it now. Did you
wish me to speak to Mr. Timms myself and show it to
him? Was that what you came in about?"

"There, didn't I say as much?" said William. "Deal
with a gent if you can get on the track of one, that's
my word. Now perhaps, George, you'll allow as I
ain't took you very far wrong tonight."

"Very well, William, very well; no need for you
to go on as if you'd 'ad to frog's-march me 'ere. I
come quiet, didn't I? All the same for that, we 'adn't
ought to take up your time this way, sir, but if it so
'appened you could find time to step round to the
company's orfice in the morning and tell Mr. Timms
what you seen for yourself, we should lay under a
very 'igh obligation to you for the trouble. You see, it
ain't bein' called—well, one thing and another, as
we mind, but if they got it into their 'ead at the
orfice as we seen things as warn't there, why, one
thing leads to another, and where we should be a

twelvemunce 'ence—well, you can understand what I mean."

Amid further elucidations of the proposition, George, conducted by William, left the room.

The incredulity of Mr. Timms (who had a nodding acquaintance with Mr. Dunning) was greatly modified on the following day by what the latter could tell and show him, and any bad mark that might have been attached to the names of William and George was not suffered to remain on the company's books, but explanation there was none.

Mr. Dunning's interest in the matter was kept alive by an incident of the following afternoon. He was walking from his club to the train, and he noticed some way ahead a man with a handful of leaflets such as are distributed to passersby by agents of enterprising firms. This agent had not chosen a very crowded street for his operation. In fact, Mr. Dunning did not see him get rid of a single leaflet before he himself reached the spot. One was thrust into his hand as he passed. The hand that gave it touched his, and he experienced a sort of little shock as it did so. It seemed unnaturally rough and hot. He looked in passing at the giver, but the impression he got was so unclear that however much he tried to reckon it up subsequently nothing would come. He was walking quickly, and as he went on glanced at the paper. It was a blue one. The name of Harrington in large capitals caught his eye. He stopped, startled, and felt for his glasses. The next instant the leaflet was twitched out of his hand by a man who hurried past and was irrecoverably gone. He ran back a few paces, but where was the passerby? And where the distributor?

It was in a somewhat pensive frame of mind that Mr. Dunning passed on the following day into the Select Manuscript Room of the British Museum and filled up tickets for Harley 3586 and some other volumes. After a few minutes they were brought to him, and he was settling the one he wanted first upon the desk when he thought he heard his own name whispered behind him. He turned round hastily and in doing so brushed his little portfolio of loose papers onto the floor. He saw no one he recognized except one of the staff in charge of the room, who nodded to him, and he proceeded to pick up his papers. He thought he had them all and was turning to begin work when a stout gentleman at the table behind him, who was just rising to leave and had collected his own belongings, touched him on the shoulder, saying, "May I give you this? I think it should be yours," and handed him a missing quire. "It is mine, thank you," said Mr. Dunning. In another moment the man had left the room. Upon finishing his work for the afternoon, Mr. Dunning had some conversation with the assistant in charge and took occasion to ask who the stout gentleman was. "Oh, he's a man named Karswell," said the assistant. "He was asking me a week ago who were the great authorities on alchemy, and of course I told him you were the only one in the country. I'll see if I can't catch him; he'd like to meet you, I'm sure."

"For heaven's sake, don't dream of it!" said Mr. Dunning. "I'm particularly anxious to avoid him."

"Oh! Very well," said the assistant. "He doesn't come here often; I daresay you won't meet him."

More than once on the way home that day Mr. Dunning confessed to himself that he did not look forward with his usual cheerfulness to a solitary evening. It seemed to him that something ill-defined and impalpable had stepped in between him and his fellowmen—had taken him in charge, as it were. He wanted to sit close up to his neighbors in the train and in the tram, but as luck would have it both train and car were markedly empty. The conductor George was thoughtful and appeared to be absorbed in calculations as to the number of passengers. On arriving at his house he found Dr. Watson, his medical man, on his doorstep. "I've had to upset your household arrangements, I'm sorry to say, Dunning. Both your servants are *hors de combat*. In fact, I've had to send them to the nursing home."

"Good heavens! What's the matter?"

"It's something like ptomaine poisoning, I should think. You've not suffered yourself, I can see, or you wouldn't be walking about. I think they'll pull through all right."

"Dear, dear! Have you any idea what brought it on?"

"Well, they tell me they bought some shellfish from a hawker at their dinnertime. It's odd. I've made inquiries, but I can't find that any hawker has been to other houses in the street. I couldn't send word to you; they won't be back for a bit yet. You come and dine with me tonight, anyhow, and we can make arrangements for going on. Eight o'clock. Don't be too anxious."

The solitary evening was thus obviated—at the expense of some distress and inconvenience, it is true. Mr. Dunning spent the time pleasantly enough with the doctor (a rather recent settler) and returned to his lonely home at about eleven thirty. The night he passed is not one on which he looks back with any satisfaction. He was in bed and the light was out. He was wondering if the charwoman would come early enough to get him hot water next morning when he heard the unmistakable sound of his study door opening. No step followed it on the passage floor, but the sound must mean mischief, for he knew that he had shut the door that evening after putting his papers away in his desk. It was rather shame than courage that induced him to slip out into the passage and lean over the banister in his nightgown, listening. No light was visible; no further sound came—only a gust of warm, or even hot, air played for an instant round his shins. He went back and decided to lock himself in his room. There was more unpleasantness, however. Either an economical suburban company had decided that their light would not be required in the small hours and had stopped working, or else something was wrong with the meter; the effect was in any case that the electric light was off. The obvious course was to find a match and also to consult his watch: he might as well know how many hours of discomfort awaited him. So he put his hand into the well-known nook under the pillow —only it did not get so far. What he touched was, according to his account, a mouth, with teeth, and with hair about it, and, he declares, not the mouth of a human being. I do not think it is any use to guess what he said or did, but he was in a spare room with the door locked and his ear to it before he was clearly conscious again. And there he spent the rest of a most miserable night, looking every moment for some fumbling at the door; but nothing came.

The venturing back to his own room in the morning was attended with many listenings and quiverings. The door stood open, fortunately, and the blinds were up (the servants had been out of the house before the hour of drawing them down); there was, to be short, no trace of an inhabitant. The watch, too, was in its usual place; nothing was disturbed, only the wardrobe door had swung open, in accordance with its confirmed habit. A ring at the back door now announced the charwoman, who had been ordered the night before, and nerved Mr. Dunning, after letting her in, to continue his search in other parts of the house. It was equally fruitless.

The day thus begun went on dismally enough. He dared not go to the Museum; in spite of what the assistant had said, Karswell might turn up there, and Dunning felt he could not cope with a probably hostile stranger. His own house was odious; he hated sponging on the doctor. He spent some little time in a call at the nursing home, where he was slightly cheered by a good report of his housekeeper and maid. Toward lunchtime he betook himself to his club, again experiencing a gleam of satisfaction at seeing the Secretary of the Association. At luncheon Dunning told his friend the more material of his woes but could not bring himself to speak of those that weighed most heavily on his spirits.

"My poor dear man," said the Secretary, "what an upset! Look here, we're alone at home, absolutely. You must put up with us. Yes! No excuse. Send your things in this afternoon."

Dunning was unable to stand out; he was, in truth, becoming acutely anxious, as the hours went on, as to what that night might have waiting for him. He was almost happy as he hurried home to pack up.

His friends, when they had time to take stock of him, were rather shocked at his lorn appearance and did their best to keep him up to the mark—not altogether without success. But when the two men were smoking alone later, Dunning became dull again. Suddenly he said, "Gayton, I believe that alchemist man knows it was I who got his paper rejected."

Gayton whistled. "What makes you think that?" he said.

Dunning told of his conversation with the Museum assistant, and Gayton could only agree that the guess seemed likely to be correct. "Not that I care much," Dunning went on, "only it might be a nuisance if we were to meet. He's a rather bad-tempered party, I imagine."

Conversation dropped again; Gayton became more and more strongly impressed with the desolateness that came over Dunning's face and bearing, and finally—though with a considerable effort—he asked him point-blank whether something serious was not bothering him. Dunning gave an exclamation of relief. "I was perishing to get it off my mind," he said. "Do you know anything about a man named John Harrington?" Gayton was thoroughly startled, and at the moment could only ask why. Then the complete story of Dunning's experiences came out— what had happened in the tramcar, in his own house, and in the street; the troubling of spirit that had crept over him and still held him; and he ended with the question he had begun with.

Gayton was at a loss how to answer him. To tell the story of Harrington's end would perhaps be right, only Dunning was in a nervous state, the story was a grim one, and he could not help asking himself whether there were not a connecting link between these two cases, in the person of Karswell. It was a difficult concession for a scientific man, but it could be eased by the phrase "hypnotic suggestion." In the end he decided that his answer tonight should be guarded; he would talk the situation over with his wife. So he said that he had known Harrington at Cambridge, and he had died suddenly in 1889, add-ing a few details about the man and his published work. He did talk over the matter with Mrs. Gayton, and, as he had anticipated, she leaped at once to the conclusion which had been hovering before him. It was she who reminded him of the surviving brother, Henry Harrington, and she also who suggested that he might be got hold of by means of their hosts of the day before.

"He might be a hopeless crank," objected Gayton.

"That could be ascertained from the Bennetts, who knew him," Mrs. Gayton retorted, and she undertook to see the Bennetts the very next day.

It is not necessary to tell in further detail the steps by which Henry Harrington and Dunning were brought together.

The next scene that does require to be narrated is a conversation that took place between the two. Dunning had told Harrington of the strange ways in which the dead man's name had been brought before him and had said something, besides, of his own subsequent experiences. Then he had asked if Harrington was disposed, in return, to recall any of the circumstances connected with his brother's death. Harrington's surprise at what he heard can be imagined, but his reply was readily given.

"John," he said, "was in a very odd state, undeniably, from time to time, during some weeks before, though not immediately before, the catastrophe. There were several things; the principal notion he had was that he thought he was being followed. No doubt he was an impressionable man, but he never had had such fancies as this before. I cannot get it out of my mind that there was ill will at work, and what you tell me about yourself reminds me very much of my brother. Can you think of any possible connecting link?"

"There is just one that has been taking shape vaguely in my mind. I've been told that your brother reviewed a book very severely not long before he died, and just lately I have happened to cross the path of the man who wrote that book in a way he would resent."

"Don't tell me the man was called Karswell."

"Why not? That is exactly his name."

Henry Harrington leaned back. "That is final to my mind. Now I must explain further. From something he said, I feel sure that my brother John was beginning to believe—very much against his will—that Karswell was at the bottom of his trouble. I want to tell you what seems to me to have a bearing on the situation. My brother was a great musician and used to run up to concerts in town. He came back three months before he died from one of these and gave me his program to look at—an analytical program—he always kept them. 'I nearly missed this one,' he said. 'I suppose I must have dropped it; anyhow, I was looking for it under my seat and in my pockets and so on, and my neighbor offered me his—said he had no further use for it—and he went away just afterward. I don't know who he was—a stout, clean-shaven man. I should have been sorry to miss it; of course, I could have bought another, but this cost me nothing.'

"At another time he told me that he had been very uncomfortable both on the way to his hotel and during the night. I piece things together now in thinking it over. Then, not very long after, he was going over these programs, putting them in order to have them bound up, and in this particular one (which, by the way, I had hardly glanced at) he found quite near the beginning a strip of paper with some very odd writing on it in red and black—most carefully done—it looked to me more like runic letters than anything else. 'Why,' he said, 'this must belong to my fat neighbor. It looks as if it might be worth returning to him; it may be a copy of something; evidently someone has taken trouble over it. How can I find his address?' We talked it over for a little and agreed that it wasn't worth advertising about, and that my brother had better look out for the man at the next concert, to which he was going very soon. The paper was lying on the book and we were both by the fire; it was a cold, windy summer evening. I suppose the door blew open, though I didn't notice it; at any rate a gust—a warm gust, it was— came quite suddenly between us, took the paper, and blew it straight into the fire. It was light, thin paper and flared and went up the chimney in a single ash. 'Well,' I said, 'you can't give it back now.' He said nothing for a minute, then rather crossly, 'No, I can't, but why you should keep on saying so I don't know.' I remarked that I didn't say it more than once. 'Not more than four times, you mean,' was all he said. I remember all that very clearly, without any good reason. And now to come to the point. I don't know if you looked at that book of Karswell's which

my unfortunate brother reviewed. It's not likely that
you should, but I did, both before his death and
after it. The first time we made game of it together.
It was written in no style at all—split infinitives and
every sort of thing that makes an Oxford gorge rise.
Then there was nothing that the man didn't swal-
low: mixing up classical myths and stories out of the
Golden Legend with reports of savage customs of
today—all very proper, no doubt, if you know how to
use them, but he didn't. He seemed to put the
Golden Legend and the *Golden Bough* exactly on a
par, and to believe both—a pitiable exhibition, in
short. Well, after the misfortune I looked over the
book again. It was no better than before, but the
impression which it left this time on my mind was
different. I suspected—as I told you—that Karswell
had borne ill will to my brother, even that he was
in some way responsible for what had happened;
and now his book seemed to me to be a very sinis-
ter performance indeed. One chapter in particular
struck me, in which he spoke of 'casting the runes'
on people, either for the purpose of gaining their
affection or of getting them out of the way—perhaps
more especially the latter. He spoke of all this in a
way that really seemed to me to imply actual
knowledge. I've not time to go into details, but the
upshot is that I am pretty sure from information received that the civil man at the concert was Karswell; I suspect—I more than suspect—that the paper
was of importance, and I do believe that if my
brother had been able to give it back he might have

been alive now. Therefore, it occurs to me to ask you whether you have anything to put beside what I have told you."

By way of answer, Dunning had the episode in the Manuscript Room at the British Museum to relate. "Then he did actually hand you some papers. Have you examined them? No? Because we must, if you'll allow it, look at them at once, and very carefully."

They went to the still-empty house—empty, for the two servants were not yet able to return to work. Dunning's portfolio of papers was gathering dust on the writing table. In it were the quires of small-sized scribbling paper which he used for his transcripts, and from one of these, as he took it up, there slipped and fluttered out into the room with uncanny quickness a strip of thin, light paper. The window was open, but Harrington slammed it to, just in time to intercept the paper, which he caught. "I thought so," he said. "It might be the identical thing that was given to my brother. You'll have to look out, Dunning; this may mean something quite serious for you."

A long consultation took place. The paper was narrowly examined. As Harrington had said, the characters on it were more like runes than anything else, but not decipherable by either man, and both hesitated to copy them, for fear, as they confessed, of perpetuating whatever evil purpose they might conceal. So it has remained impossible (if I may anticipate a little) to ascertain what was con-

veyed in this curious message or commission. Both
Dunning and Harrington are firmly convinced that
it had the effect of bringing its possessors into very
undesirable company. That it must be returned to
the source whence it came they were agreed, and
further, that the only safe and certain way was that
of personal service; and here contrivance would be
necessary, for Dunning was known by sight to Karswell. He must, for one thing, alter his appearance
by shaving his beard. But then might not the blow
fall first? Harrington thought they could time it.
He knew the date of the concert at which the "black
spot" had been put on his brother: it was June 18.
The death had followed on September 18. Dunning
reminded him that three months had been mentioned on the inscription on the car window. "Perhaps," he added with a cheerless laugh, "mine may
be a bill at three months, too. I believe I can fix it
by my diary. Yes, April twenty-third was the day
at the Museum; that brings us to July twenty-third.
Now, you know, it becomes extremely important to
me to know anything you will tell me about the
progress of your brother's trouble, if it is possible for
you to speak of it."

"Of course. Well, the sense of being watched
whenever he was alone was the most distressing
thing to him. After a time I took to sleeping in his
room, and he was the better for that; still, he talked
a great deal in his sleep. What about? Is it wise
to dwell on that, at least before things are
straightened out? I think not, but I can tell you

this: two things came for him by post during those weeks, both with a London postmark and addressed in a commercial hand. One was a woodcut of Bewick's, roughly torn out of the page—one which shows a moonlit road and a man walking along it, followed by an awful demon creature. Under it were written the lines out of the 'Ancient Mariner' (which I suppose the cut illustrates) about one who, having once looked round—

'walks on,
And turns no more his head,
Because he knows a frightful fiend
Doth close behind him tread.'

The other was a calendar such as tradesmen often send. My brother paid no attention to this, but I looked at it after his death and found that everything after September eighteenth had been torn out. You may be surprised at his having gone out alone the evening he was killed, but the fact is that during the last ten days or so of his life he had been quite free from the sense of being followed or watched."

The end of the consultation was this: Harrington, who knew a neighbor of Karswell's, thought he saw a way of keeping a watch on his movements. It would be Dunning's part to be in readiness to try to cross Karswell's path at any moment, to keep the paper safe and in a place of ready access.

They parted. The next weeks were no doubt a severe strain upon Dunning's nerves; the intangible barrier which had seemed to rise about him on the day when he received the paper gradually developed into a brooding blackness that cut him off from the means of escape to which one might have thought he might resort. No one was at hand who was likely to suggest them to him, and he seemed robbed of all initiative. He waited with inexpressible anxiety as May, June, and early July passed on for a mandate from Harrington. But all this time Karswell remained immovable at Lufford.

At last, less than a week before the date he had come to look upon as the end of his earthly activities, came a telegram: "Leaves Victoria by boat train Thursday night. Do not miss. I come to you tonight. Harrington."

He arrived accordingly, and they concocted plans. The train left Victoria at nine and its last stop before Dover was Croydon West. Harrington would mark down Karswell at Victoria and look out for Dunning at Croydon, calling to him if need were by a name agreed upon. Dunning, disguised as far as might be, was to have no label or initials on any hand luggage and must at all costs have the paper with him.

Dunning's suspense as he waited on the Croydon platform I need not attempt to describe. His sense of danger during the last days had only been sharpened by the fact that the cloud about him had perceptibly been lighter, but relief was an ominous symptom, and if Karswell eluded him now, hope was gone, and there were so many chances of that. The rumor of the journey might be itself a device. The twenty minutes in which he paced the platform and persecuted every porter with inquiries as to the boat train were as bitter as any he had spent. Still, the train came, and Harrington was at the window. It was important, of course, that there should be no recognition, so Dunning got in at the farther end of the corridor carriage and only gradually made his way to the compartment where Harrington and Karswell were. He was pleased, on the whole, to see that the train was far from full.

Karswell was on the alert but gave no sign of recognition. Dunning took the seat not immediately facing him and attempted, vainly at first, then with increasing command of his faculties, to reckon the possibilities of making the desired transfer. Opposite Karswell and next to Dunning was a heap of Karswell's coats on the seat. It would be of no use to slip the paper into these—he would not be safe, or would not feel so, unless in some way it could be proffered by him and accepted by the other. There was a handbag, open and with papers in it. Could he manage to conceal this (so that perhaps Karswell might leave the carriage without it) and then find and give it to him? This was the plan that suggested itself. If he could only have counseled with Harrington! But that could not be. The minutes went on. More than once Karswell rose and went out into the corridor. The second time Dunning was on the point of attempting to make the bag fall off the seat, but he caught Harrington's eye and read in it a warning. Karswell, from the corridor, was watching— probably to see if the two men recognized each other. He returned but was evidently restless, and

when he rose the third time hope dawned, for
something did slip off his seat and fall with hardly
a sound to the floor. Karswell went out once more
and passed out of range of the corridor window.
Dunning picked up what had fallen and saw that
the key was in his hands in the form of one of
Cook's ticket cases, with tickets in it. These cases
have a pocket in the cover, and within very few
seconds the paper of which we have heard was in
the pocket of this one. To make the operation more
secure, Harrington stood in the doorway of the compartment and fiddled with the blind. It was done
and done at the right time, for the train was now
slowing as it approached Dover.

In a moment more Karswell reentered the compartment. As he did so, Dunning, managing he knew
not how to suppress the tremble in his voice, handed
him the ticket case, saying, "May I give you this,
sir? I believe it is yours." After a brief glance at the
ticket inside, Karswell uttered the hoped-for
response. "Yes it is; much obliged to you, sir," and
he placed it in his breast pocket.

Even in the few moments that remained—moments of tense anxiety, for they knew not to what a
premature finding of the paper might lead—both men
noticed that the carriage seemed to darken about
them and to grow warmer; that Karswell was fidgety
and oppressed; that he drew the heap of loose coats
near him and cast it back as if it repelled him; and
that he then sat upright and glanced anxiously at
both. They, with sickening anxiety, busied them-

selves in collecting their belongings, but they both thought that Karswell was on the point of speaking when the train stopped at Dover Town. It was natural that in the short space between town and pier they should both go into the corridor.

At the pier they got out, but so empty was the train that they were forced to linger on the platform until Karswell should have passed ahead of them with his porter on the way to the boat, and only then was it safe for them to exchange a pressure of the hand and a word of concentrated congratulation. The effect upon Dunning was to make him almost faint. Harrington made him lean up against the wall, while he himself went forward a few yards within sight of the gangway to the boat, at which Karswell had now arrived. The man at the head of it examined his ticket, and, laden with coats, he passed down into the boat. Suddenly the official called after him, "You, sir. Beg pardon, did the other gentleman show his ticket?" "What the devil do you mean by 'the other gentleman'?" Karswell's snarling voice called back from the deck. The man bent over and looked at him. "The devil? Well, I don't know, I'm sure," Harrington heard him say to himself, and then aloud, "My mistake, sir; must have been your rugs! Ask your pardon." And then, to a subordinate near him, "'Ad he got a dog with him, or what? Funny thing, I could 'a' swore 'e wasn't alone. Well, whatever it was, they'll 'ave to see to it aboard. She's off now. Another week and we shall be gettin' the 'oliday customers." In five minutes more there was nothing but the lessening lights of the boat, the long line of the Dover lamps, the night breeze, and the moon.

Long and long the two sat in their room at the Lord Warden. In spite of the removal of their greatest anxiety, they were oppressed with a doubt, not of the lightest. Had they been justified in sending a man to his death, as they believed they had? Ought they not to warn him, at least? "No," said Harrington, "if he is the murderer I think him, we have done no more than is just. Still, if you think it better—but how and where can you warn him?" "He was booked to Abbeville only," said Dunning. "I saw that. If I wired to the hotels there in Joanne's Guide, 'Examine your ticket case—Dunning,' I should feel happier. This is the twenty-first; he will have a day. But I am afraid he has gone into the dark." So telegrams were left at the hotel office.

It is not clear whether these reached their destination, or whether, if they did, they were understood. All that is known is that on the afternoon of July 23 an English traveler, examining the front of St. Wulfram's Church at Abbeville, then under extensive repair, was struck on the head and instantly killed by a stone falling from the scaffold erected round the northwestern tower, there being, as was clearly proved, no workman on the scaffold at that moment; and the traveler's papers identified him as Mr. Karswell.

Only one detail shall be added. At Karswell's sale a set of Bewick, sold with all faults, was acquired by Harrington. The page with the woodcut of the traveler and the demon was, as he had expected, mutilated. Also, after a judicious interval, Harrington repeated to Dunning something of what he had heard his brother say in his sleep, but it was not long before Dunning stopped him.

The Book

Margaret Irwin

ON A FOGGY night in November Mr. Corbett, having
guessed the murderer by the third chapter of his
detective story, arose in disappointment from his bed
and went downstairs in search of something more
satisfactory to send him to sleep.

The fog had crept through the closed and curtained
windows of the dining room and hung thick on the
air, in a silence that seemed as heavy and breathless
as the fog.

The dining-room bookcase was the only considerable one in the house and held a careless, unselected
collection to suit all the tastes of the household,
together with a few dull and obscure old theological
books that had been left over from the sale of a
learned uncle's library. Cheap red novels bought on
railway stalls by Mrs. Corbett, who thought a journey
the only time to read, were thrust in like pert, under-
sized intruders among the respectable nineteenth
century works of culture, chastely bound in dark
blue or green, which Mr. Corbett had considered
the right thing to buy during his Oxford days; beside
these, there swaggered the children's large, gaily

bound storybooks and collections of fairy tales in every color.

From among this neat new clothbound crowd there towered here and there a musty sepulcher of learning, brown with the color of dust rather than leather, with no trace of gilded letters, however faded, on its crumbling back to tell what lay inside. A few of these moribund survivors from the dean's library were inhospitably fastened with rusty clasps; all remained closed and appeared impenetrable— their blank, forbidding backs uplifted above their frivolous surroundings with the air of scorn that belongs to a private and concealed knowledge.

It was an unusual flight of fancy for Mr. Corbett to imagine that the vaporous and fog-ridden air that seemed to hang more thickly about the bookcase was like a dank and poisonous breath exhaled by one or another of these slowly rotting volumes.

He hurriedly chose a Dickens from the second shelf as appropriate to a London fog and had returned to the foot of the stairs when he decided that his reading tonight should by contrast be of blue Italian skies and white statues, in beautiful rhythmic sentences. He went back for a Walter Pater.

He found *Marius the Epicurean* tipped sideways across the gap left by his withdrawal of *The Old Curiosity Shop.*

It was a very wide gap to have been left by a single volume, for the books on that shelf had been closely wedged together. He put the Dickens back into it and saw that there was still space for a large book. He said to himself, in careful and precise words, "This is nonsense. No one can possibly have gone into the dining room and removed a book while I was crossing the hall. There must have been a gap before in the second shelf." But another part of his mind kept saying, in a hurried, tumbled torrent, "There was no gap in the second shelf."

He snatched at both the *Marius* and *The Old Curiosity Shop* and went to his room in a haste that was unnecessary and absurd.

Tonight, Dickens struck him in a different light. Beneath the author's sentimental pity for the weak and helpless he could discern a revolting pleasure in cruelty and suffering, while the grotesque figures of the people in Cruikshank's illustration revealed too clearly the hideous distortions of their souls. What had seemed humorous now appeared diabolic, and in disgust at these two old favorites he turned to Walter Pater for the repose and dignity of a classic spirit.

But presently he wondered if this spirit were not in itself of a marble quality, frigid and lifeless, contrary to the purpose of nature. "I have often thought," he said to himself, "that there is something evil in the austere worship of beauty for its own sake." He had never thought so before, but he liked to think that this impulse of fancy was the result of mature consideration, and with this satisfaction he composed himself for sleep.

He woke two or three times in the night, an unusual occurrence, but he was glad of it, for each

time he had been dreaming horribly of these blame-
less Victorian works.

When he had wakened in a cold sweat, he decided
there was nothing for it but to go down and get
another book that would turn his thoughts in some
more pleasant direction. But his increasing reluctance
to do this found a hundred excuses. The recollection
of the gap in the shelf now recurred to him with a
sense of unnatural importance; in the troubled dozes
that followed, this gap between two books seemed
the most hideous deformity, like a gap between the
front teeth of some grinning monster.

But in the clear daylight of the morning Mr. Corbett came down to the pleasant dining room, to its
sunny windows and smell of coffee and toast, and
ate an undiminished breakfast with a mind chiefly
occupied in self-congratulation that the wind had
blown the fog away in time for his Saturday game
of golf. Whistling happily, he was pouring out his
final cup of coffee when his hand remained arrested
in the act, as his glance, roving across the bookcase,
noticed that there was now no gap at all in the
second shelf. He asked who had been at the bookcase already, but neither of the girls had, nor Dicky,
and Mrs. Corbett was not yet down. The maid never
touched the books. They wanted to know what book
he missed in it, which made him look foolish, as he
could not say.

"I thought there was a gap in the second shelf," he
said, "but it doesn't matter."

"There never is a gap in the second shelf," said

little Jean brightly. "You can take out lots of books from it, and when you go back the gap's always filled up. Haven't you noticed that? I have."

Nora, the middle one in age, said Jean was always being silly; she had been found crying over the funny pictures in the *Rose and the Ring* because she said all the people in them had such wicked faces.

Mr. Corbett did not like to think of such fancies for his Jeannie. She retaliated briskly by saying Dicky was just as bad, and he was a big boy. He had kicked a book across the room and said, "Filthy stuff," just like that. Jean was a good mimic; her tone expressed a venom of disgust, and she made the gesture of dropping a book as though the very touch of it were loathsome. Dicky, who had been making violent signs at her, now told her she was a beastly little sneak, and he would never again take her for rides on the step of his bicycle. Mr. Corbett was disturbed as he gravely asked his son how he had got hold of this book.

"Took it out of that bookcase, of course," said Dick furiously.

It turned out to be the *Boy's Gulliver's Travels* that Granny had given him, and Dicky had at last to explain his rage with the devil who wrote it to show that men were worse than beasts and the human race a washout.

Mr. Corbett, with some annoyance, advised his son to take out a nice, bright, modern boy's adventure story that could not depress anybody. It appeared, however, that Dicky was "off reading just now," and the girls echoed this.

Mr. Corbett soon found that he, too, was "off reading." Every new book seemed to him weak, tasteless, and insipid, while his old and familiar books were depressing or even, in some obscure way, disgusting. Authors must all be filthy-minded; they probably wrote what they dared not express in their lives.

His taste for reading revived as he explored with relish the hidden infirmities of minds that had been valued by fools as great and noble. He saw Jane Austen and Charlotte Brontë as two unpleasant examples of spinsterhood: the one as a prying, subacid busybody in everyone else's flirtations, the other as a raving, craving maenad seeking self-immolation on the altar of her frustrated passions.

These powers of penetration astonished him. With a mind so acute and original he should have achieved greatness, yet he was a mere solicitor and not prosperous at that. If he had but the money he might do something with those ivory shares, but it would be a pure gamble, and he had no luck. His natural envy of his wealthier acquaintances now mingled with a contempt for their stupidity that approached loathing. The digestion of his lunch in the City was ruined by meeting sentimental yet successful dotards, whom he had once regarded as pleasant fellows. The very sight of them spoiled his game of golf, so that he came to prefer reading alone in the dining room even on sunny afternoons.

He discovered also, and with a slight shock, that

Mrs. Corbett had always bored him. Dicky he began actively to dislike as an impudent blockhead, and the two girls were as insipidly alike as white mice; it was a relief when he abolished their tiresome habit of coming in to say good night.

In the now unbroken silence and seclusion of the dining room he read with feverish haste, as though he were seeking for some clue to knowledge, some secret key to existence which would quicken and inflame it.

He even explored the few decaying remains of his uncle's theological library. One of these books had diagrams and symbols in the margin, which he took to be mathematical formulas of a kind he did not know. He presently discovered that they were drawn, not printed, and that the book was in manuscript, in a very neat, crabbed black writing that resembled black letter printing. It was, moreover, in Latin, a fact that gave Mr. Corbett a shock of unreasoning disappointment. For while examining the signs on the margin he had been filled with an extraordinary exultation, as though he knew himself to be on the edge of a discovery that should alter his whole life. But he had forgotten his Latin.

With a secret and guilty air which would have looked absurd to anyone who knew his harmless purpose, he stole to the schoolroom for Dicky's Latin dictionary and grammar and hurried back to the dining room, where he tried to discover what the book was about with an anxious industry that surprised himself. There was no name to it, nor of the author. Several blank pages had been left at the end, and the writing ended at the bottom of a page, with no flourish nor superscription, as though the book had been left unfinished. From what sentences he could translate, it seemed to be a work on theology.

There were constant references to the Master, to his wishes and injunctions, which appeared to be of a complicated kind. Mr. Corbett began by skipping these as mere accounts of ceremonial, but a word caught his eye as one unlikely to occur in such an account. He read this passage attentively, looking up each word in the dictionary, and could hardly believe the result of his translation.

"Clearly," he decided, "this book must be by some early missionary and the passage I have just read the account of some horrible rite practiced by a savage tribe of devil worshippers." Though he called it "horrible," he reflected on it, committing each detail to memory. He then amused himself copying the signs in the margin near it and trying to discover their significance. But a sensation of sickly cold came over him, his head swam, and he could hardly see the figures before his eyes. He suspected a sudden attack of influenza and went to ask his wife for medicine.

They were all in the drawing room, Mrs. Corbett helping Nora and Jean with a new game, Dicky playing the Pianola, and Mike, the Irish terrier, who had lately deserted his accustomed place on the dining-room hearthrug, stretched by the fire.

He thought how like sheep they looked and sounded. Nothing in his appearance in the mirror struck him as odd: it was their gaping faces that were unfamiliar. He then noticed the extraordinary behavior of Mike, who had sprung from the hearth-rug and was crouched in the farthest corner uttering no sound, but with his eyes distended and foam round his bared teeth. Under Mr. Corbett's glance, he slunk toward the door, whimpering in a faint and abject manner, and then as his master called him he snarled horribly, and the hair bristled on the scruff of his neck.

"What *can* be the matter with Mike?" asked Mrs. Corbett.

Her question broke a silence that seemed to have lasted a long time. Jean began to cry. Mr. Corbett said irritably that he did not know what was the matter with any of them.

Then Nora asked, "What is that red mark on your face?"

He looked again in the glass and could see nothing.

"It's quite clear from here," said Dicky. "I can see the lines in the fingerprint."

"Yes, that's what it is," said Mrs. Corbett in her brisk, staccato voice, "the print of a finger on your forehead. Have you been writing in red ink?"

Mr. Corbett precipitately left the room for his own, where he sent down a message that he was suffering from a headache and would have his dinner in bed. He wanted no one fussing round him. By next morning he was amazed at his fancies of influenza, for he had never felt so well in his life.

No one commented on his looks at breakfast, so that he concluded the mark had disappeared. The old Latin book he had been translating on the previous night had been moved from the writing bureau, although Dicky's grammar and dictionary were still there. The second shelf was, as always in the daytime, closely packed; the book had, he remembered, been in the second shelf. But this time he did not ask who put it back.

That day he had an unexpected stroke of luck in a new client of the name of Crab, who entrusted him with large sums of money; nor was he irritated by the sight of his more prosperous acquaintances, but with difficulty refrained from grinning in their faces, so confident was he that his remarkable ability must soon place him higher than any of them. At dinner he chaffed his family with what he felt to be the gaiety of a schoolboy.

In spite of this new alertness he could not attend to the letters he should have written that evening and drifted to the bookcase for a little light distraction, but found that for the first time there was nothing he wished to read. He pulled out a book from above his head at random, and saw that it was the old Latin book in manuscript.

As he turned over its stiff and yellow pages, he noticed with pleasure the smell of corruption that had first repelled him in these decaying volumes, a smell, he now thought, of ancient and secret knowledge.

This idea of secrecy seemed to affect him personally, for on hearing a step in the hall he hastily closed the book and put it back in its place. He went to the schoolroom, where Dicky was doing his homework, and told him he required his Latin grammar and dictionary again for an old law report. To his annoyance he stammered and put his words awkwardly; he thought that the boy looked oddly at him and he cursed him in his heart for a suspicious young devil, though of what he should be suspicious he could not say. Nevertheless, when back in the dining room, he listened at the door and then softly turned the lock before he opened the books on the writing bureau.

The script and Latin seemed much clearer than on the previous evening, and he was able to read at random a passage relating to a trial of a German midwife in 1620 for the murder and dissection of 783 children.

It appeared to be an account of some secret society whose activities and ritual were of a nature so obscure, and when not, so vile and terrible, that Mr. Corbett would not at first believe that this could be a record of any human mind.

He read until far later than his usual hour for bed, and when at last he rose, it was with the book in his hands. To defer his parting with it, he stood turning over the pages until he reached the end of the writing, and was struck by a new peculiarity.

The ink was much fresher and of a far poorer quality than the thick, rusted ink in the bulk of the book; on close inspection he would have said that it was of modern manufacture and written quite recently, were it not for the fact that it was in the same crabbed late seventeenth century handwriting.

This, however, did not explain the perplexity, even dismay and fear, he now felt as he started at the last sentence. It ran: *Continue te in perennibus studiis,* and he had at once recognized it as a Ciceronian tag that had been dinned into him at school. He could not understand how he had failed to notice it yesterday.

Then he remembered that the book had ended at the bottom of a page. But now the last two sentences were written at the very top of a page. However long he looked at them, he could come to no other conclusion than that they had been added since the previous evening.

He now read the sentence before the last—*Re imperfecta mortuus sum*—and translated the whole as "I died with my purpose unachieved. Continue, thou, the never-ending studies."

With his eyes still fixed upon it, Mr. Corbett replaced the book on the writing bureau and stepped back from it to the door, his hand outstretched behind him, groping and then tugging at the door handle. As the door failed to open, his breath came in a faint, hardly articulate scream. Then he remembered that he had himself locked it, and he fumbled with the key in frantic, ineffectual movements until at last he opened it and banged it after him as he plunged backward into the hall.

For a moment he stood there looking at the door handle; then, with a stealthy, sneaking movement, his hand crept out toward it, touched it, began to turn it, when suddenly he pulled his hand away and went up to his bedroom, three steps at a time.

There he hid his face in the pillow, cried and raved in meaningless words, repeating, "Never, never, never. I will never do it again. Help me never to do it again." With the words "Help me," he noticed what he was saying—they reminded him of other words, and he began to pray aloud.

But the words sounded jumbled; they persisted in coming into his head in a reverse order, so that he found he was saying his prayers backward, and at this final absurdity he suddenly began to laugh very loud. He sat up on the bed, delighted at this return to sanity, common sense, and humor, when the door leading into Mrs. Corbett's room opened, and he saw his wife staring at him with a strange, gray, drawn face that made her seem like the terror-stricken ghost of her usually smug and placid self.

"It's not burglars," he said irritably. "I've come to bed late, that is all, and must have wakened you."

"Henry," said Mrs. Corbett, and he noticed that she had not heard him: "Henry, didn't you hear it?"

"What?"

"That laugh."

He was silent, an instinctive caution warning him to wait until she spoke again. And this she did, imploring him with her eyes to reassure her.

"It was not a human laugh. It was like the laugh of a devil."

He checked his violent inclination to laugh again. It was wiser not to let her know that it was only his laughter she had heard. He told her to stop being fanciful, and Mrs. Corbett gradually recovered her docility.

The next morning Mr. Corbett rose before any of the servants and crept down to the dining room. As before, the dictionary and grammar alone remained on the writing bureau; the book was back on the second shelf. He opened it at the end. Two more lines had been added, carrying the writing down to the middle of the page. They ran:

> *Ex auro canceris*
> *In dentem elephantis.*

Which he translated as:

> Out of the money of the crab
> Into the tooth of the elephant.

From this time on, his acquaintances in the City noticed a change in the mediocre, rather flabby and unenterprising "old Corbett." His recent sour depression dropped from him; he seemed to have grown twenty years younger, strong, brisk, and cheerful, and with a self-confidence in business that struck them as lunacy. They waited with a not unpleasant excitement for the inevitable crash, but his every speculation, however wild and harebrained, turned out successful.

He never stayed in town for dinners or theaters,

for he was always now in a hurry to get home, where, as soon as he was sure of being undisturbed, he would take down the manuscript book from the second shelf of the dining room and turn to the last pages.

Every morning he found that a few words had been added since the evening before, and always they formed, as he considered, injunctions to himself. These were at first only with regard to his money transactions, giving assurance to his boldest fancies, and since the brilliant and unforeseen success that had attended his gamble with Mr. Crab's money in African ivory, he followed all such advice unhesitatingly.

But presently, interspersed with these commands, were others of a meaningless, childish, yet revolting character, such as might be invented by a decadent imbecile.

He at first paid no attention to these directions, but found that his new speculations declined so rapidly that he became terrified not merely for his fortune but for his reputation and even safety, since the money of various of his clients was involved. It was made clear to him that he must follow the commands in the book altogether or not at all, and he began to carry out their puerile and grotesque blasphemies with a contemptuous amusement, which, however, gradually changed to a sense of their monstrous significance. They became more capricious and difficult of execution, but he now never hesitated to obey blindly, urged by a fear he could not understand.

By now he understood the effect of this book on the others near it and the reason that had impelled its mysterious agent to move the books into the second shelf, so that all in turn should come under the influence of that ancient and secret knowledge.

In respect to it, he encouraged his children, with jeers at their stupidity, to read more, but he could not observe that they ever now took a book from the dining-room bookcase. He himself no longer needed to read, but went to bed early and slept soundly. The things that all his life he had longed to do when he should have enough money now seemed to him insipid. His most exciting pleasure was the smell and touch of these moldering pages as he turned them to find the last message inscribed to him.

One evening it was in two words only: *Canem occide.*

He laughed at this simple and pleasant request to kill the dog, for he bore Mike a grudge for his change from devotion to slinking aversion. Moreover, it could not have come more opportunely, since in turning out an old desk he had just discovered some packets of rat poison bought years ago and forgotten. He whistled lightheartedly as he ran upstairs to rummage for the packets and returned to empty one in the dog's dish of water in the hall.

That night the household was awakened by terrified screams proceeding from the stairs. Mr. Corbett was the first to hasten there, prompted by the instinctive caution that was always with him these days. He saw Jean, in her nightdress, scrambling up onto the landing on her hands and knees, clutching at anything that afforded support and screaming in a choking, tearless, unnatural manner. He carried her to the room she shared with Nora, where they were quickly followed by Mrs. Corbett.

Nothing coherent could be got from Jean. Nora said that she must have been having her old dream again. When her father demanded what this was, she said that Jean sometimes woke in the night, crying, because she had dreamed of a hand passing backward and forward over the dining-room bookcase until it found a certain book and took it out of the shelf. At this point she was always so frightened that she woke up.

On hearing this, Jean broke into fresh screams, and Mrs. Corbett would have no more explanations. Mr. Corbett went out onto the stairs to find what had brought the child there from her bed. On looking down into the lighted hall he saw Mike's dish overturned. He went down to examine it and saw that the water he had poisoned must have been upset and absorbed by the rough doormat, which was quite wet.

He went back to the little girls' room, told his wife that she was tired and must go to bed, and he would now take his turn at comforting Jean. She was now much quieter. He took her on his knee, where at first she shrank from him. Mr. Corbett remembered with an awed sense of injury that she never now sat on his knee and would have liked to pay her out for it by mocking and frightening her. But he had to coax her into telling him what he wanted, and with this object he soothed her, calling her by pet names that he thought he had forgotten, telling her that nothing could hurt her now he was with her. He listened to what he had at last induced her to tell him.

She and Nora had kept Mike with them all the evening and taken him to sleep in their room for a treat. He had lain at the foot of Jean's bed and they had all gone to sleep. Then Jean began her old dream of the hand moving over the books in the dining-room bookcase, but instead of taking out a book it came across the dining room and out onto the stairs. It came up over the banisters and to the door of their room and turned their door handle very softly and opened it. At this point she jumped up, wide awake, and turned on the light, calling to Nora. The door, which had been shut when they went to sleep, was wide open, and Mike was gone.

She told Nora that she was sure something dreadful would happen to him if she did not go and bring him back, and ran down into the hall, where she saw him just about to drink from his dish. She called to him and he looked up, but did not come, so she ran to him and began to pull him along with her when her nightdress was clutched from behind and then she felt a hand seize her arm.

She fell down and then clambered upstairs as fast as she could, screaming all the way.

It was now clear to Mr. Corbett that Mike's dish must have been upset in the scuffle. She was again crying, but this time he felt himself unable to comfort her. He retired to his room, where he walked up and down in an agitation he could not understand.

"I am not a bad man," he kept saying to himself. "I have never done anything actually wrong. My clients are none the worse for my speculations, only the better."

Presently he added, "It is not wrong to try and kill a dog, an ill-tempered brute. It turned against me. It might have bitten Jeannie."

He noticed that he had thought of her as Jeannie, which he had not done for some time; it must have been because he had called her that tonight. He must forbid her ever to leave her room at night; he could not have her meddling. It would be safer for him if she were not there at all.

Again that sick and cold sensation of fear swept over him; he seized the bedpost as though he were falling and held on to it for some minutes. "I was thinking of a boarding school," he told himself, and then, "I must go down and find out—find out—" He would not think what it was he must find out.

He opened his door and listened. The house was quiet. He crept onto the landing and along to Nora and Jean's door, where again he stood listening. There was no sound, and at that he was again overcome with unreasonable terror. He imagined Jean lying very still in her bed—too still. He hastened away from the door, shuffling in his bedroom slippers along the passage and down the stairs.

A bright fire still burned in the dining-room grate. A glance at the clock told him it was not yet twelve.

He stared at the bookcase. In the second shelf was a gap which had not been there when he had left. On the writing bureau lay a large open book. He knew that he must cross the room and see what was written in it. Then, as before, words that he did not intend came sobbing and crying to his lips, muttering, "No, no, not that. Never, never, never." But he crossed the room and looked down at the book. As last time, the message was in only two words: *Infantem occide*.

He slipped and fell forward against the bureau. His hands clutched at the book, lifted it as he recovered himself, and with his finger he traced out the words that had been written. The smell of corruption crept into his nostrils. He told himself that he was not a sniveling dotard but a man stronger and wiser than his fellows, superior to the common emotions of humanity, who held in his hands the sources of ancient and secret power.

He had known what the message would be. It was after all the only safe and logical thing to do. Jean had acquired dangerous knowledge. She was a spy, an antagonist. That she was so unconsciously, that she was eight years old, his youngest and favorite child, were sentimental appeals that could make no difference to a man of sane reasoning power such as his own.

Jean had sided with Mike against him. "All that are not for me are against me," he repeated softly. He would kill both dog and child with the white powder that no one knew to be in his possession.

He laid down the book and went to the door. What he had to do he would do quickly, for again that sensation of deadly cold was sweeping over him. He wished he had not to do it tonight; last night it would have been easier, but tonight she had sat on his knee and made him afraid. He imagined her lying very still in her bed—too still.

He held on to the door handle, but his fingers seemed to have grown numb, for he could not turn it. He clung to it, crouched and shivering, bending over it until he knelt on the ground, his head beneath the handle which he still clutched with upraised hands. Suddenly the hands were loosened and flung outward with the frantic gesture of a man falling from a great height, and he stumbled to his feet.

He seized the book and threw it on the fire. A violent sensation of choking overcame him; he felt he was being strangled; as in a nightmare he tried again and again to shriek aloud, but his breath would make no sound. His breath would not come at all. He fell backward heavily down on the floor, where he lay very still.

In the morning the maid who came to open the dining-room windows found her master dead. The sensation caused by this was scarcely so great in the City as that given by the simultaneous collapse of all Mr. Corbett's recent speculations. It was instantly assumed that he must have had previous knowledge of this and so committed suicide.

The stumbling block of this theory was that the

medical report defined the cause of Mr. Corbett's death as strangulation of the windpipe by the pressure of a hand which had left the marks of its fingers on his throat.

Whitman CLASSICS

The Hound of the
  Baskervilles

Tales to Tremble By

More Tales to Tremble By

Seven Great Detective
  Stories

Black Beauty

Tales From Arabian Nights

Little Women

The Call of the Wild

Tom Sawyer

Robin Hood

The Wonderful Wizard
  of Oz

Robinson Crusoe

Wild Animals I Have
  Known

The War of the Worlds

Stand By for Adventure

Huckleberry Finn

Alice in Wonderland

REG. U.S. PAT. OFF.

*Start your home library of
WHITMAN CLASSICS now.*

Whitman ADVENTURE and MYSTERY Books

SPORTS STORIES

Throw the Long Bomb!

Hot Rod Road

THE POWER BOYS

The Burning Ocean

The Vanishing Lady

The Million-Dollar Penny

ADVENTURE TALES

Tarzan of the Apes

The Return of Tarzan

Tarzan and the City
of Gold

Tarzan and the Lost Safari

The Space Eagle

. . . .

Walt Disney
The Gnome-Mobile
Blackbeard's Ghost

TELEVISION FAVORITES

Bonanza
Killer Lion
Treachery Trail

Garrison's Gorillas

Lassie
Secret of Smelters' Cave
Secret of the Summer
Bristlecone Pine
Wild Mountain Trail

The Monkees

Rat Patrol

Star Trek

Man From U.N.C.L.E.
Gunrunners' Gold
Gentle Saboteur

I Spy

F Troop

The Invaders

The Big Valley